Grace

Grace

Vanessa Smith

QUATTRO BOOKS

The publication of *Grace* has been generously supported by the Canada Council for the Arts and the Ontario Arts Council.

Cover art: Photography by Diane Mascherin
Cover design: Diane Mascherin
Author's photo: Mathieu Beaudoin
Typography: Grey Wolf Typography
Editors: Beatriz Hausner and John Calabro

Library and Archives Canada Cataloguing in Publication

Smith, Vanessa
    Grace / Vanessa Smith.

ISBN 978-1-926802-26-8

    I. Title.

PS8637.M56595G73 2011   C813'.6   C2010-907663-X

Novella Series #17
Published by Quattro Books Inc.
89 Pinewood Avenue
Toronto, Ontario, M6C 2V2
www.quattrobooks.ca

Printed in Canada

For my family. You are my heart.

CHAPTER ONE

"Can I help you find something, dear?" she asks, from atop a spindly-legged stool. Short and squat, she hooks her truncated limbs over the highest set of rungs. Her knitting flows forth onto the hard packed dirt floor, a pink woollen waterfall cascading over her abundant belly.

"No, thank you," I reply, continuing to browse. I hate questions like this. It makes all the fine, lightly browned hairs on the back of my neck stand up. I hate them almost as much as I hate help, particularly from strangers. "I'm just looking."

"Well, I can see that," she says, "but what is it you're looking *for*?" She plucks a pair of glasses from her nose and rests them on her floral-covered bosom. She smoothes out her bird's nest mane of yellowish-white hair, expertly whipping it into a bun and securing it with a spare needle. "You can't find what you want if you don't know what you need."

I murmur my assent, but don't meet her gaze. I don't want to encourage the press of her familiarity, and I silently curse myself for leaving my visit so late. Earlier, the aisles of the Flea Market would have been full of prospective buyers; but, at this hour, the crowds have thinned considerably. She smells a sale and launches herself in my direction.

"As you can see," she says, "I've got something for everyone, dear. All kinds of nice things."

Mm-hmm. She does − not necessarily nice − but things nonetheless. Her kick-stand table is piled high with brooches, books, buttons and other bric-a-brac − a strange assortment of items that have even less charm than they do worth. However, as I glance over her wares, I'm drawn to one piece in particular − a cameo pendant − a softly pearled profile set in calcified curls. I lift it from the table, running my fingers over the slightly raised image. It reads like Braille, giving rise to a memory so old I almost have to blow the dust from it.

My Nana gave my sister a pendant very much like this once. It was Rachel's birthday. She was thirteen and wore the piece with a budding womanly pride. I was five and filled with childishness and envy. She guarded it as though it were the Crown Jewels − unclasping it and placing it carefully on her nightstand each evening before she went to bed. I was forbidden from touching it. She said I'd dirty it − the filigreed face − and that I was too young to understand. She was wrong. *She* didn't understand. All I wanted to do was hold it.

One morning, I took it without asking, pocketing the pendant before kindergarten for Show-and-Tell. I knew it wasn't mine to either show *or* tell, but I didn't care. The secret weight of its presence in my pocket made me feel like someone special − the transporter of important goods − even if they weren't mine. Naturally, I later lost it in a schoolyard game of hide-and-go-seek.

Rachel was livid, and nothing could convince her that I wasn't the guilty culprit. Of course, I lied, and even constructed a paperclip chain to replace it; however, this act of contrition only bought me clemency from my parents. Rachel accepted the offering − she had no choice − but I don't think she ever quite believed me, nor forgave me.

I cringe, and the chain slips from my fingers. I love memories, but this has turned to one of fetid shame and I don't want to linger there. I forget the face. Forget Rachel. Return to browsing. To my right, a mountain of satin brassieres forms a series of domed foam peaks, towering at least a foot taller than my 5'10" frame. They spill out over the edge of the table in a mess of clasps and straps, and I look up in awe and wonderment.

"Is it a brassiere you're looking for, love?" she asks, catching me staring. "I can fix you right up!"

"No," I reply, mortified. My pale cheeks flush as pink as hers. "I just…"

"Let's see," she says, appraising my chest. "Well, dear, you certainly aren't blessed, are you? But," she says, "what you lack up top, you more than make up for in leg room." She laughs, running her eyes the length of me. "Now, let's see what we can do for your little lady friends. What do I have on the petite side?" She rummages through the beige heap and sets loose a lingerie landslide. "Aha! You're in luck!" she cries. "I just picked up a surplus from a friend in Chinatown – just the ticket!"

"Please, don't…," I say. "I'm not looking for a bra."

"Oh," she says, the sense of urgency in my voice staying her hands. She turns, womanly wares dripping from her fingers like dirty dishwater. "Well, what then, dear? I have it all. And my goods are all above board," she says, casting a furtive glance around her, "not like some others…"

I follow her gaze across the aisle where some tables are buried beneath electronics, hastily ripped-out wires like the snarled roots of an unearthed shrub. Two middle-aged men guard their loot – both slight and heavily tattooed in soiled white undershirts. They share a cigarette and an early supper of hot dogs and French fries.

"The people they let in here nowadays," she says, clicking her tongue in disapproval. "This used to be a respectable establishment. I've been coming here twenty years back, you know; I can assure you – you can trust Faye."

She beams up at me, laying a pudgy palm on my forearm. Her touch is hot and hard, and its subtle insistency makes me uncomfortable. She seems nice enough; but then, nothing is ever what it seems here – a place where worthless artefacts are pawned off as priceless antiques.

"So, what is it you want, my dear?"

"I don't know," I reply, sidestepping her grasp. "But I'll know when I find it." In truth, I know exactly what I'm looking for and I've already spotted it – a small innocuous-looking shoe box underneath her table. I can see the telltale cache of serrated white edges peeking out, self-evident in the semi-darkness. "What about those?" I ask, pointing behind her. "Right there."

"Which, love?" she says, spinning on her heels. "Oh, those...those are just some old photos from a neighbour of mine. Well, not *her* really – she passed away, poor thing; but the young man, the son – he didn't know what to do with them. I told him I'd take them off his hands. Try to make a few dollars for him if he liked. Just trying to be charitable, you know."

"Can I see them?"

"Oh, certainly...certainly," she replies, eager to acquiesce now that she's cottoned on to the tail of my desire. She retrieves the box and sweeps away a sea of baubles to make room on the tabletop. "Are you interested in photography, dear?"

Yes, I am interested, but I don't let on. I don't want to betray the slightest hint of curiosity as it might raise the worth of an otherwise worthless item. I can feel Faye studying my profile as I flip through the photos. She crosses her arms squarely over her chest and launches into another of her sales pitch soliloquies.

"I could swear I've seen you somewhere before," she says, squinting. She sets her glasses on her redly veined nose. "I could just *swear*. Do you come here often, dear?"

Yes, I haunt this hall most Sunday afternoons; however, I have to be vague. These people – the sellers – they can sense someone like me…a collector. They know the desperation that accompanies obsession and how to leverage it to their advantage. "No," I reply, "not really."

"Well, I must be mistaken then, but we don't see many pretty young girls like you in this old place," she says, gesturing towards the iron rafters. "What brings you here?"

"Do you know anything about these photos?" I ask, attempting to divert her attention. "Other than what you've already told me."

"Oh, they're nothing special," she says, craning her head around the curve of my elbow. "Just a few leftovers from an old lady's life – old, like me," she chuckles. She's interrupted then by the electronic trill of a cell phone, ringing beneath the pile of pink wool. "Oh, that's me," she says. "Pardon me. Just wait one moment, dear – just hold on *one* moment."

Grateful for the distraction, I nod and feign a smile, not at her, but at her choice of words. Some moments are meant to be caught – held in your hand a little longer. Some are not. I only know because I collect them – not moments, but pictures of them – photographs. I've been doing this since I was a child and my collection's quite big now – mostly black-and-whites. These are my favourites. Some are people that I know, but most are not. It all started with my Nana. She used to let me have her outtakes – the images that didn't develop perfectly. Once I grew up, I discovered that most flea markets sell old photographs. This realization was a defining moment. It's when I became a true collector.

The images I've amassed aren't special per se – just ordinary pictures of ordinary people with ordinary lives. I don't know anything about them. I don't know their names or what they do or how they're related. In fact, the only thing I can discern for certain is the mood, which is how I organize my collection: emotively. I store them in shoe boxes on a wooden bank of shelves in my bedroom. Their corresponding labels inked on the front. Admiration. Anticipation. Gratitude. Happiness.

Hope. Joy. Pride. Serenity. Surprise. Wonder. Those are just a few. Most of the boxes are for good emotions, the so-called "happy" ones. No one ever seems to take sad photos or photos of sadness. These are very rare – the sad kind – very hard to come by.

I rifle through Faye's collection and find that it's a standard mix. Celebrations. Birthdays. Picnics. Dinners. And then, one that's less easy to categorize, sandwiched between two images of smiling women arm in arm. A solitary figure on the shore, fronting a line of stripy-backed tents with sun loungers peeking out. She wears a sheer white shirt. It's long – conceals her wrists – but not the U-shaped curves of her bikini clad bottom. A heavily beaded necklace rests on her chest, and a pair of sandals dangle from her left hand. Her right is raised above a pair of dark glasses – running precisely parallel to the sea. She's looking out at something…or someone…searching the horizon. One foot is buried in the sand, and the other is bent flamingo-like across the front of her body. Her entire frame seems to lean into the sea, as though poised and ready – prepared to take flight or swim away.

I pull the photo from the box and hold it at arm's length. Study it more closely. *Who is she?* I have an irresistible desire to see her face, but it's hidden – partially obscured by the large floppy brim of a sun hat. Shading her face. Shielding her from me. *What is she looking at? What is she looking for?*

"Okay, okay…" Faye says, chatting away at her phone. "I heard you."

I slip the photo of the woman back into the box and take a deep breath. I have a sudden urge to swipe the box and make a run for it, hoping to avoid the inevitable bargaining process. I always hate this part, mostly because I've never considered myself a very good bluffer. Already I can feel butterflies beginning to fill my stomach and I shift nervously from one foot to the other. Wait for her to finish.

"...right, right," she says. "Okay, I'll see you then, love. Bye, bye, now." Faye wraps up her call with a definitive snap of her wrist, flipping the phone closed.

I pounce immediately, hoping to catch her off guard, and attempt to adopt a studied air of nonchalance that doesn't telegraph my intentions. "So, how much for these?" I ask. "I mean, roughly..."

"Those? Well," she says, "I hadn't given it much thought, dear. What would they be worth to you?"

"Not much," I reply. "I use them for scrap. You know, art and stuff."

"Ah," she replies. "You young people – always up to something." She hooks a hand over the edge of the box and drags it back towards her, pink press-on nails pulling the photos from my reach. I feel a slight catch in my throat – the faintest hint of fear that Faye will not play ball.

"I could take them all," I reply. "You know, get them out of your hair."

"Well, let's see," she says. "If you take the whole box, I suppose I could give it to you for – oh, thirty dollars."

"I can give you ten," I try. "Photos like these are easy enough to find."

Faye fidgets. Checks her watch. "Let's make it fifteen then," she says. "I'm not sure I could give that poor boy much less for his dead mother's photographs, dear. You know how these things are..."

I do. She's played her strongest hand – the guilt card – but I'm unmoved. In my years of bartering for photos, I've heard worse tales than that of Faye's undoubtedly fictitious dead "friend." Besides, I'm used to women like her. Women that trade in emotional manipulation. My mother is like this. And so is Rachel. I've been dealing with them for nearly twenty-two years now. *This is a game I can play.*

"I'll give you ten," I repeat. "That's all I've got." As proof, I produce a worn bill from my pocket, and Faye fixes her eyes on it, fretting over the gold watch on her wrist.

"Fine, fine," she says, snatching at the bill. She spirits it away, tucking it into the white strap of her bra. She pushes the box towards me and I lift it from the table, cradling it against my hip.

"There now, dear – all's well that ends well," she says, dusting her hands together. "I'm sure I don't need to tell you, but you've done that boy a real favour – a *real* favour." She pats my arm appreciatively but I recoil, stepping back. "What kind of art is it you do, dear? If you don't mind my asking…"

I do. People are always asking me this question. They ask me why I collect photos; and, over the years, I've found that the shortest answer is often simplest. The safest. "Nothing special," I reply. "It's just a hobby. That's all."

"Oh…" Faye says, suddenly silenced. Her face falls into a puckered pout, and I briefly consider indulging her. I could tell her the real reason that I collect photographs. I could tell her that I like their significance – the fact that someone, somewhere, thought that something in the images was worth saving – worth seeing. I could say I consider it my personal obligation to honour that sentiment. To look at the people, and let them know, *I see you, even if no one else can*. I could tell her all these things, but I don't. I've never liked explaining myself, least of all to strangers.

"Well," she replies, "you're sure I can't interest you in anything else? If it's pictures you're after, I've got a real nice collection of postcards here." She directs my attention to a plastic tub of glossy images – brightly coloured 4"x 6" windows on the world. Dublin. New York. Key West. Tokyo. Omaha. Amsterdam. Madrid. "An artistic young lady such as yourself," she says, "I'm sure you'd find a use for them. I could even give you a special price, since you seem so fond of photos."

"No, thank you," I say, without pause for consideration. "I'm not interested." I already have a collection of these – postcards with politely worded paternal sentiments penned from around the world. They've come in a steady stream since I was eight – since my father first left – and I have no desire to add to this collection. It's large enough already.

"Right then," she says, "I best let you be on your way. It's getting late and we're closing up."

I glance around and see that she's right – the hall now empty of all but vendors. A lone figure in tan coveralls moves between the tables, pushing a wide broom, sweeping up the day's debris – paper hot dog holders and cast-off peanut shells.

"Yes, you're right," I reply. "I better get going, but thanks. For the photos, I mean."

"Oh, it's my pleasure," she coos, her face brightening at my indication of gratitude. "You come back any time, you hear. I'll remember you, dear. If ever I get any more pictures, I'll remember. That's one thing about me. I never forget a face, dear. Faye *never* forgets a face."

"Thank you," I repeat, eager to be gone. "I appreciate it."

"As I said, I'm Faye," she reminds me, thrusting a pudgy forearm towards me. "And you are?"

I shift the box to the other hip, hesitantly extending my right hand. She grips it between both of hers, patting the top in an uncomfortably intimate way. I've never liked the touch of a stranger's skin. It makes me self-conscious. It reminds me that fingertips have feelings and I never fail to wonder what they feel when they feel me.

"I'm Grace," I say. "My name is Grace."

"Grace!" she repeats. "That's a beautiful name, dear. A beautiful name for a beautiful girl. You *look* like a Grace. So tall and elegant – so graceful. It suits you perfectly!"

"Thank you," I reply, tugging at my hand. "I better go though. I'll miss my bus."

"Oh, of course," she says, releasing me. "Good-bye, Grace. I'll see you soon!"

I turn and slip between the tables, sneaking out a side door. The gravel-lined parking lot is filled with vans and RVs, each butted up against the corrugated metal wall. Ten foot tall white lettering peeks over the top, spelling out VANCOUVER FLEA MARKET. In the distance, the late spring sun is just beginning to set behind the crystalline dome of Main Street's Science World; and, overhead, the SkyTrain rattles along Terminal Avenue, a treeless industrial thoroughfare that runs the length of the train station.

I'm the only foot traffic; this area of Vancouver so devoid of life that even the homeless don't make their homes here. I decide it must be about seven o'clock. I have no way of knowing for sure, as I never wear a watch. But then, I hate time – mostly because I'm never on it. Which is yet another thing I love about my photos – the absence of time – their timelessness.

I like that the occupants never age, no matter how old they get. I like the way everything stays precisely where I left it. The way the feelings never falter. Eternal emotions – sensations fixed forever in photo paper. Eternal joy. Eternal triumph. Eternal pride. Eternal love. Eternal happiness. The photographer only captures that one brilliant image – the single second when everyone simply smiles, or pretends to at least, for posterity's sake. I like this – the pure and utter ignorance of what comes next. Eternal innocence. Eternal bliss.

I grip the box even closer to my chest and head west, picking my way over the cracked concrete of the sidewalk. I make a beeline for the bus stop, quickening my pace – heading towards home. I'll have to hurry. I've promised to meet Ilena later tonight and she'll never let me hear the end of it if I'm late for the show.

CHAPTER TWO

I slip through the back gate, careful to silence the tell-tale *thud*. The lights of night are just beginning to come on, and the first dark fingers of dusk filter through the trees. In the dark, I mingle with the cornucopia of ferns and rhododendrons – shaded from sight by the shaggy mammoths that line the thatched network of Kitsilano's streets. These are mostly perennials. In the summer, their leafy parasols shroud the narrow car-lined avenues in darkness. In the winter, their stark black limbs tangle themselves in Vancouver's cloud-filled sky. Laughter trips out into the garden, fragments of speech and sound, indistinct as they sift through the screen. The sleepy clink of a knife laid to rest on the edge of a porcelain plate. The delicate jangle of a bracelet on a wrist. The delighted slap of a tightly denim-clad thigh. The unmistakable murmur of voices. Rachel's laugh follows close on the heels of a joke I cannot hear – punctuating a punch line I'm not privy to. I climb the back stairs, cocking my hip to hold the box, as I pull the door open. I step into the soft square of orange light that illuminates the kitchen, uncomfortable in my uncertainty as to what lies beyond. *I didn't know we were having guests*; but then, Rachel never tells me anything.

"Grace," she cries, "you're here!" She smiles up at me from the vinyl banquette – a simple gesture that sets my pulse pounding with suspicion. Rachel's stingy with her smiles at the best of times, and doesn't usually waste one on me. Intuition tells me something isn't right, but I have no time to figure out what.

"Where were you?" she asks. "I left a message on your phone."

"Out," I reply, "at the Flea Market."

"Oh, right," she says, "Sunday." She laughs, and her cheeks belie the subtle blush of dinner party drunkenness. I release my hold on the screen door and it swings shut with a hoarse metallic sigh, forcing me to advance even farther into the room.

"Say hello to everyone," she orders, casting her arms wide. "Be sociable."

I set the box down on the edge of the banquette and scan the faces – mostly familiar – Eric and Melissa, both old friends of Rachel's. The fourth face, a boy's, is foreign, but I sense I've seen it before. Rachel catches me staring.

"You've met Will, haven't you?" she asks. "He's Melissa's..." Her sentence trails off as she attempts to describe someone who wouldn't be around long enough to merit memory.

"Her what?" Eric laughs – a deep set of dimples laughing along with him.

"My man slave," Melissa chimes in, sliding a hand down Will's chest. The air is thick with marijuana and the walls are coated with the heavy scent of curry. I feel suddenly sober and self-conscious – firmly planted outside something I can't seem to slip into.

"Oh, of course," I reply, trying to regain some ground, "I think we met last month...at Rachel's birthday party." I can say this with some degree of self-assurance, confident at least in my memory of that evening – confident in Rachel's as well. Watching her face, I see the barb hit home, knocking the wind out of her high-spirited sails. Suddenly stoic, she smoothes a hand over her darkly bobbed chin-length hair. Tucks it behind her left ear. This is a habit of hers. She always does it when she's angry or uncomfortable. The table falls silent, except for

Eric, who makes a noisy show of stretching his arms above his head.

"Yeah, that was some party, Rach," he says. "You really know how to ring in the big three-oh." He settles back into place and brings his wine glass to his lips, awkwardly swigging something which should be sipped. His eyes meet mine across the table but I avoid his gaze, my cheeks burning with indignation at his clumsy attempt to save me, or perhaps himself. After all, it's not as though I was alone when Rachel walked in on us. As though I'm the only guilty party.

Even today, I defend my innocence. It wasn't my fault. Rachel was the one who had insisted I attend her party, despite my objections. I told her I'd be the youngest by ten years. Told her I'd have nothing to say to her PhD-wielding friends. But she wouldn't listen. Said I was her sister so I should be there; and so, I was.

I remember that night well, despite one too many glasses of red wine. After a few disappointing attempts to mingle, I'd set up shop in the kitchen where I spent the evening cutting up limes and cheering on a tequila competition between Eric and another guest. He was the only person I knew, other than Melissa of course; however, by that time, she was already tongue-deep in a conversation with Will. As the night wore on, the intoxicating effects of the alcohol fanned the flames of what felt like mutual desire. Through eyes glazed and glassy, everything glowed a little more warmly. Laughs laughed louder, and hands lingered longer over legs.

Deep down, I knew Eric was only taking pity on my party pariah status, but I didn't mind. It felt nice to be noticed, even in that small inconsequential way. And so, we found a dimly-lit corner – a room just off the hall – and while the remaining guests cleaned up crumbs and broken bottles, I loosened belt buckles and unzipped zippers. Showed off one of my few natural talents; until, of course, Rachel walked in and ruined everything. I still don't understand why she got so upset. It's not as though we slept together. It was just a blow job. That's all. I had no desire to sleep with Eric. Still don't. Have no desire to sleep with anyone as a matter of fact.

Don't get me wrong. I've slept with men before – well, boys really. Throughout university, I'd engaged in a few drunken dalliances, but these interactions had all been brief and unsatisfying. I remember hearing girls talk about *going all the way*. I used to wonder what it meant. What it felt like. *All the way to where? To what?* All the sex I'd ever had never seemed like a final destination. Just groping hands on tender breasts. The impersonal probes of friends of other friends. A few short thrusts and then it was done. Over time, I'd learned there were other ways to seek gratification, ones I didn't need men or their manhood for – although I'd still been known to make exceptions...I had for Eric, at least.

In the end, I wasn't surprised when he was forgiven right away. I was not so lucky; but then, I don't have his squeaky-clean track record. This is the trouble with sisters – mine anyway. They never forget. And you can forget about forgive.

"It's too bad you missed dinner," Melissa says, keen to cut the tension. "It was really good." She gestures towards the table, now set with dirty plates and stemware stained with red wine rings. Rachel sips hers slowly. Silently. I try to gauge her mood but she's inscrutable.

"I didn't realize you were having a party," I reply. "Rachel never told me."

"Well, it's not a party really," Melissa replies. "We just ordered some Indian – threw something together." She waves her hand around as though conjuring the cardboard boxes from thin air. "You know, a Bon Voyage type of thing."

"Bon Voyage?" I ask. "Who's leaving?"

"What do you mean?" she says, smiling back at me. "Rachel, of course."

"What?" I reply, turning back to Rachel. "What are you talking about? Where?"

"Toronto," Rachel says. "I've got an interview for a teaching position there – U of T."

"Isn't that great?" Melissa chirps, clapping her hands together. "Her first choice!" Rachel has wanted to teach Economics back east for as long as I can remember. She's never liked Vancouver. Thinks anything worth happening happens in Toronto.

"Anyway," Rachel interjects, "I have to go there for the interview, so I had to book a flight right away. It was all so last minute. I didn't have time to mention it. I leave tomorrow."

"Tomorrow?" I ask. "So soon?"

"They wanted to see me ASAP," she says. "The post is for the fall. Someone just announced their leave, and my old supervisor recommended me to the Hiring Committee. She thinks I might be able to slip through the back door." She says this so casually, with no regard for the full implications of the words themselves – uprooting her life and moving halfway across the country.

"And, what then?" I ask. "What about the house? What about all this?" I don't say it, but what I really want to ask is, *What about me?* I've been living rent-free in Rachel's attic for four years – since I first started university – a deal she'd struck with my mother who had agreed to pay part of Rachel's mortgage if she'd put up with me. Watch out for me.

"Nothing's for sure yet," she says, "but if I do get it, I'll have to move, yes." Her eyes meet mine and my breath comes shorter in my chest. I struggle to match her self-composure.

"You could have told me," I shoot back. "You could've said something." Even as I say this, I know that it's redundant. She couldn't have seen this coming. *Or could she?* Either way, I'm grasping at straws of self-righteousness and I know it. I feel suddenly afraid – a raw gnawing fear that tastes like the tang of rusted metal on the back of my tongue. I try to remember the last time I tasted fear like this. Not for a while. Probably not since the initial uncertainty of my parents' divorce. *What will this mean for me?* That question has always given birth to a selfish primal fear – the one that only surfaces when some basic need for food or shelter is being threatened.

"Let's not talk about it right now," Rachel says. "We'll cross that bridge when we come to it."

Sure. I set my jaw in anger and frustration – pettiness and resentment welling up in the back of my throat like a wad of rubber bands. What she means is that *she* will cross that bridge when she comes to it, making the decisions with no thought as to how they will affect me. She'll cross the bridge and burn it behind her, heading east over the Rockies.

"If you need to reach me," she says, "I'll be staying at Dad's."

"Dad's in town?" I ask, my attention suddenly diverted as she utters the magic word. "He's home – in Toronto?"

"No, of course not," she replies. "He's out of the country – Argentina or somewhere."

"Jesus," Melissa says, "your dad has the sweetest gig ever. I'd kill to fly around the world on other people's dime."

"It's not like he travels for fun," I retort. "It's work-related." This is true; but then, so is Melissa's remark. Our father is a retired law professor – a late-in-life environmental consultant who prospects mining sites for legal pitfalls or run-ins with activist groups. It keeps him busy. And away a lot. "He has to travel," I say. "It's his job."

"Right," Rachel says, "sipping wine and warding off Greenpeace. He's a real humanitarian." She brings a conspiratorial hand close to her mouth, shielding me from her next statement which she utters loudly enough for me to hear. "Don't mind Grace," she says. "She likes to think of our father as a rebel with a cause. He's basically just a retiree with a company credit card."

Everyone laughs. Tries to lighten the suddenly sombre mood. Everyone but me.

"You know, you sound more and more like Mom every day, Rachel," I reply. "I mean, that's not exactly new material, is it?" The table falls silent, and I feel vindicated, having defended my dad's honour. He'd never ask me to, but I get so sick of it – the same jokes – especially when my father is always the first to laugh at himself. Rachel and my mother are always the last.

"That reminds me," Rachel says, barely missing a beat, "I need your help with Mom."

"What?" I ask, trying to adjust to the turning tide of the conversation. It seems Rachel is always moving beyond my ken, one step ahead. "Help with what?"

"With Mom," she repeats. "I bought her those tickets for Mother's Day, remember? To that concert at the Chan Centre. You'll have to take her."

I run my hand over my hair, pulling the ruddy waves taut across my temples, trying to buy myself some time. My immediate response is a resounding *No!* But it isn't the concert I object to. I love classical music. Rachel and I were raised on the stuff, absorbing an appreciation for it as though by osmosis. And so, it isn't the free concert I could do without. It's my mother. Or, more specifically, the thought of spending upwards of two unmediated hours with her – her and her pert opinions about my life's direction, or lack thereof. "Can't she go with someone else?" I ask, fishing for an alternative. "I have a life too."

"Grace," Rachel says, "it's Mother's Day. Don't be difficult, okay. Just do it."

I cross my arms over my chest, resolved to stand firm, but I feel cornered – trapped – not wanting to look too obstinate or childish in front of Rachel's friends. "Fine," I say. "I'll do it – since I have no choice. When is it anyway?"

"Saturday," she says. "I'll leave the tickets in the front hall. Don't forget them. And don't be late. Oh, and one more thing," she says, scarcely drawing breath. "I need you to drive me to the airport tomorrow."

"I can't," I reply. "I have to work. It's my first shift of the summer. I can't miss it."

"Give me a break, Grace. It's just the coffee shop," she says. "What time are you done?"

"3:30."

"Perfect," she says. "My flight's not 'til 6:00."

I want to object, but Rachel, as usual, has removed all objections. "Fine," I reply. "I'll do it."

"Thank you," she says, smiling. I seem to have temporarily won her favour and her countenance softens to its former semi-drunk consistency. "Here," she says, "sit down. Have a drink with us." She pats the seat beside her as though I were a dog but she doesn't move over.

"No, thanks," I reply, heading towards the hallway. "I'm going out again. I just wanted to change."

"Where are you going?"

I ignore her and continue up the stairs.

"Grace!" she calls again. "I asked you a question."

"What?!"

"I asked you a question," she repeats. "Where are you going?"

It would be so simple to answer, but I can't bring myself to do it. She never tells me anything; and yet, my life is supposed to be transparent. *It's not fair.* Even after four years, I'm still the little sister – still tracked – still tailed. Still a second-class citizen in my own home.

"Grace," she calls, "did you hear me?"

I pause, my foot poised to mount the second set of stairs. Sigh. Give up. Give in. "Celebrities!" I shout, conceding defeat. "I'm going to Celebrities."

CHAPTER THREE

"Grace," Ilena cries, "over here!" She stands beside the curb outside the club, her platinum blonde head hanging off the fringes of the crowd. I hand the taxi driver a twenty and don't bother asking for change. I've always felt cowed by the assertiveness of cabbies. Besides, tonight, I don't care. I'm eager to be gone – to get in, to get drunk. I slip between the cracks of the club-goers, inching my way towards Ilena. I find her planted firmly on the wrong side of the bouncer-backed velvet rope.

"Finally," she cries, holstering a rhinestone-encrusted cell phone. She shoots me a nasty look. "Where were you? I've been waiting for almost half an hour."

"I know. I know. I'm sorry," I reply. "It's Rachel."

"Ah," Ilena says, "of course. What was it tonight?"

"Never mind," I reply. "I don't want to talk about it."

"Fine," she says, shrugging a set of deeply tanned shoulders. "Suit yourself."

"You look great," I say, "as usual." Ilena is a self-professed fashion addict who often foregoes purchasing groceries to feed her shopping addiction. Tonight, she's wearing a black leather mini dress with neon yellow squares peeping through the windows of laser-cut frames, a pair of black stilettos wound round her ankles. She's still short – at least, shorter than me;

but I've never failed to feel dwarfed by her personal dynamism. Ilena's everything I'm not – a snappy spitfire with dangerous curves – rounded with an edge.

"I see I still haven't converted you to my cause," she says. "More vintage?" She gives me a disparaging glance, taking in my sleeveless black sheath – simple and unadorned. It's silk – a lucky score from my favourite second-hand shop.

"No," I reply, "but maybe one day."

"How many times have I heard that?" she asks. "*One day*, I'll get my fashionable hands on you, Grace Linde. I swear to God."

"I think you'd be wasting your time," I reply. "I could never pull *that* off. I'm a little more...subtle."

"Bullshit," Ilena laughs. "Everyone likes attention. And besides, I'm not telling you to wear a fucking 'For Sale' sign around your neck. It just wouldn't hurt to attract a little more attention to yourself – you know, a little more *male* attention."

"Well, if that's your objective then what the hell are we doing here?" I laugh. Celebrities sits on Davie Street, right in the heart of the gay village. It serves as central HQ for local revellers, home to myriad queens, queers and all variety of hangers-on. Ilena and I are the latter.

"RuPaul, darling," she laughs. "One night only. I wouldn't miss her for the world."

"What gives anyway?" I ask. "Why can't we go in?"

"Seriously, I know," Ilena says. "I'm not going to wait out here all night. I need a fucking drink. I mean, don't we deserve one? Hail the conquering graduates!"

I laugh, but I'm the only one. In the crowd of mostly gay men, no one takes any notice of Ilena – a fairly rare occurrence.

Ilena is my best friend. She's also my only friend – at least, the only one that I share more than a convivial acquaintance with. We met at UBC in first-year Spanish class. Bonded instantly over our shared linguistic ineptitude and our mutual appreciation for our professor's Barcelonian buttocks. Over the years, we'd kept pace with one another, both deciding to major in art history, although our studies followed different streams. Last week was our long-awaited convocation.

"Now you're attracting *unwanted* attention," I reply. "Let's just get inside."

"Yeah, let's get me drunk," she cries. "God, where is that brother of mine?"

"You mean, you haven't seen him yet?"

"No, but all the other usual suspects are here."

I glance around, scanning the sidewalk. Seventy-five percent gay guys and twenty-five percent straight girls. *The usual suspects.* The guys come for the music and the half-naked go-go dancers. The girls come for half-priced Smirnoff Ice and freedom from the dance floor advances of drunken straight males. There are turf wars from time to time; but the two groups tend to co-exist in harmony, rarely at cross purposes.

"Lots of girls tonight," I say. "I think our secret's out."

"No shit," Ilena replies. "Fuck it. These girls are all posers anyway. At least we have an *in.*" The "in" that Ilena refers to is her older brother, Pavel. He's the reason we've been conferred straight girl diplomatic immunity. By day, he works as a straight-laced investment banker for Toronto Dominion. By night, he moonlights as a drag queen named Ophelia Cox. Ilena and I have shared presidency of the fan club for the past four years.

"I guess they're RuPaul fans too," I reply, shrugging my shoulders in their unsolicited defence.

"Well, it's Sunday," she says. "Probably the industry crowd – servers that had to work all weekend. Anyway, I don't care who they are. I don't do lines. Can you see my brother?"

Looking around, I spot Ophelia near the doors, waving regally to the crowd and soaking up a smattering of pre-show applause. "There she is," I cry. "Ophelia!"

"Darlings!" she cries, beckoning us forward. "This way!" Ilena shoves me forward into the sea of protesting fans, but Ophelia raises her hand to command silence. At nearly seven feet tall, she is a force to be reckoned with and we're permitted to pass. We duck beneath the rope and she wraps us in an aromatic embrace, bending down to deliver four air kisses – one to each of our cheeks. "I was just beginning to wonder where you were."

"We couldn't get in," Ilena replies. "This place is a madhouse. What time does she go on?"

"Not until 11:30, but I'm on at 11:00," Ophelia says. "I'm so nervous I could die. I mean, it's fucking RuPaul!" She guides us through the double doors, stooping down low to avoid lopping off her yellow tresses, the curls cascading down over her thin shoulders.

"What number are you doing?" I ask. "Something new?"

"Of course not!" she says, bringing a demure hand to her décolletage. "I wouldn't dream of trying new material tonight, you silly girl! I'm doing a classic, darlings – Nancy Sinatra."

"Well, you're certainly dressed for it," Ilena says. I steal a glance at Ophelia's ensemble as she chats with Ilena. She's the perfect member of Sinatra's sixties mod-squad – red patent leather boots – the four-inch platforms nearly painted on. These complement a pair of red sequined shorts and a too-small white tube top.

"Have you been raiding Ilena's closet again?" I ask with a smile, secretly envying her ability to let it all hang out. To be herself so brazenly. So boldly.

"No, yours, you little bitch!" Ophelia replies. She laughs and bats my arm, pulls me closer towards her. "Look, girls – I have to dash. I'm on in ten," she says. "So scoot! Get yourselves a drink, and you tell that cocksucker, Dominic, he better put it on my tab." She pushes us towards the packed bar, and disappears into the crowd, a blonde cork bobbing along in a sea of strangers.

"So, what'll it be?" Ilena asks, twining her arm through mine. "Something worthy of celebration...how about champagne!?"

"Sure," I reply. "You're in charge tonight."

"No way," she says. "We're both celebrating. You're not getting off the hook that easy."

"I'm not trying to," I reply. "But let's face it, you're the only one with cause to celebrate." Ilena had just won a full scholarship to Columbia to do her Masters in curatorial studies. She'd be going to New York in the fall. "No one exactly rolls out the red carpet for completing a B.A. these days," I say. "Besides, I'm just happy it's over."

"God, me too," Ilena says. "I thought we'd never see the end of that place. I'm so excited to get the fuck out of here."

I laugh. Try to smile. For Ilena's sake at least. Try not to think about how much I'm going to miss her.

"You know, you could still come with me," she says. "To New York, I mean." She raises an eyebrow in silent expectation. "Even just for the summer. You can stay with me and my aunt. Help me find a place for fall. I mean, how can you say *no*, Grace? It's New York! The Guggenheim. MOMA. The Met. It's all there! Everything."

"I already told you," I reply, "I can't."

"Why?" she asks. "Give me one good reason."

"I have a life here, Ilena. I can't just pick up and leave," I say. "What about all my stuff?"

"Your stuff?" she asks. "Leave it. It'll be here when…*if*…you get back. And if not, you get new stuff. Trust me, *stuff* is easier to come by than experiences of a lifetime."

"Well, maybe I'll come for a visit later on," I try. "After you get set up." She looks unconvinced, but I stand firm, despite the fact that I don't know why. I'd only have to pay for my plane ticket. New York. Free room and board. *Why can't I say yes?* It's a question that teeter-totters in my mind with no balance or ballast. For two weeks now, I've been searching for an answer, or simply a counterweight to fear.

"So, *what* then?" she asks. "What'll you do in the fall if you don't come with me?"

"Weren't we supposed to be getting drinks?" I ask, pointing toward the bar. "Surely that's more important than a rundown of my five-year life plan."

"Fine, fine," she laughs. "Ply me with liquor! Okay, drinks first. Then, dance floor." She shimmies up to the bar, slipping seamlessly between two occupied stools. Unlike me, Ilena's successfully able to insert herself anywhere. I'm too awkward. Too tall.

She returns and shoves a flute of champagne towards me. Grips my arm and elbows her way out onto the dance floor. The swell of the crowd forces us to the left of the stage where we stake our claim. The other concert-goers press close, and my thin frame rubs up against half-naked strangers in the sudden crush of bodies. Everyone is smiling and sweaty and sweet-smelling, and the air is filled with after-shave applied with a too heavy hand. Beside me, Ilena tilts her head back, and drains her glass.

"You know," I yell, "you're not supposed to chug champagne."

"Bottoms up!" she says, shrugging her shoulders. "You said I was in charge."

I narrow my eyes at her and consider sipping the rest of my champagne in a slow lady-like fashion simply to infuriate her, but I think better of it. Tip the glass skyward, the bubbles burning all the way down.

"Here," she says, "give me your glass. One more before Ophelia's set."

"No!" I reply, wiping tears from my eyes desperate for relief from the panting heat of the crowd. "I'll go. You stay."

"Fine," she says. "Your funeral."

Shit. The line at the bar is at least three people deep, and I have to squeeze myself between two shirtless men with matching rainbow suspenders and handlebar moustaches. I attempt to flag Dominic down, but I can barely bring my arm away from my side. I'm stuck. Sardined into obscurity.

"Can I help you?" a voice behind me asks. I turn, and the first thing I notice is his height. He's tall. I only know because I rarely have to look up. Usually, men are looking up at me.

"Sorry, what?" I ask, cupping my hand close to my ear, not certain I heard him correctly.

"Can I help you?" he repeats. "Are you trying to get a drink?"

"Yes," I laugh, "although I think I might have more luck if I were a man."

"Possibly," he says. "Here, allow me." He leans over a few patrons and flags down a passing bartender. "What'll it be?" he asks me.

"Champagne," I reply, "two glasses, please."

"Two glasses of champagne," he says, flashing a grin. It has the intended effect, and the bartender disappears beneath the counter. He brandishes a bottle, giving it a dramatic shake to rile up the crowd, and onlookers cheer their encouragement as he makes a show of popping the cork. I hang back. I wait. *We* wait.

After his height, the second thing I notice is his age. He's old – at least, older than me, and certainly much older than the usual Celebrities set. I wonder if he's here for the concert or if he's a regular – possibly on a date – or looking for one. Gay or straight...he's handsome – not "hot," as Ilena would say – but handsome in that obnoxious unjust way that older men grow ever more sexy as everything about them grows ever less the same. The kind of man that cleans up well, easy and elegant in a graceless sort of way.

"Here you go," he says. "Two glasses of champagne." He hands them off to me, and places a hand on the small of my back, guiding me through the crowd like a ship's rudder. We step away from the bar but not each other, finding some room to breathe.

"Thanks," I reply, raising my glass in his direction. "You're a lifesaver."

"Don't mention it," he says. "It's my pleasure."

Damn. I want to say something witty or sexy but can't think of anything. Instead, I just smile.

"So," he says, "I notice you're not a gay guy."

"Yes," I reply, "I'm merely an imposter."

"Glad to hear it," he says. "Maybe you can offer a few pointers to an accidental tourist."

"Is this your first time here?"

"Guilty as charged," he replies. "I'd never set foot in this place before tonight."

"Are you here with your boyfriend?" I ask. "Or a date...or something?"

"No, nothing like that," he laughs. "I'm not gay actually. My friend, she did the promo for the show tonight, and we were on our way back from dinner. She just wanted to pop in."

"God, I'm sorry," I reply. "I thought you might be – I mean, I just assumed that you were..." I feel my cheeks flush red. "Why didn't you say something?"

"Say what?" he asks. "Should I have had, *Hey, I'm not gay* stamped on my forehead at the door? Besides, you were being ignored. I was just trying to be a gentleman."

"Oh, well...thanks," I reply, still embarrassed by my error. "But you should have said something."

"Are you always this grateful to men who try to be nice to you?" he asks. "I hate to see what would happen if I did something really horrible like buy you dinner."

"Oh, God! That reminds me," I say. "You didn't pay for these, did you?"

"As a matter of fact, I did," he replies, "but don't worry. It was nothing."

"But they were supposed to be taken care of," I say. "We have a tab."

"A tab?" he repeats, raising an eyebrow. "Come here often?"

"My friend's brother performs here," I say. "Our drinks are usually taken care of. Anyway, you shouldn't have paid."

"Well, you can make it up to me some other time."

"Are you sure?"

He nods. Smiles. Winks.

"Well, thanks again for your help."

"Not to worry," he says. "I'm always happy to be of service to a beautiful woman."

I blush deeply then, and pray he can't see me for the dark. Take a sip of champagne and savour the moment a little longer. I'm flattered by his attention, but not sure what to do with it. No one has ever referred to me as a woman before, and it feels strange and insincere, despite its apparent accuracy. "I should go," I reply. "My friend's waiting for me."

"Of course," he says. "I won't keep you."

"Well, maybe I'll see you later," I reply, gesturing to the stage. "I mean, out there..."

"Maybe," he says, smiling. "Maybe not."

I turn to walk away, intent on finding Ilena; but, glancing back, I see he's still standing there – staring at me – the weight of his gaze falling soft and fuzzy on my shoulders. I allow the feeling of being admired for admiration's sake to wash over me. Allow the awareness of some latent power warming my insides as the champagne bubbles ripple through my blood.

CHAPTER FOUR

Somewhere, an alarm clock cries an insistent double *chirrup*. Slow-moving messages traverse my nervous system, telegraphing pain to every fibre. My heart beats behind my eyes and inside the end of each fingertip. I prop myself up and lean over the edge of my bed to silence the alarm. It lies on the floor, half-buried beneath last night's hastily shed skin. As I bend down, a host of images swim before my eyes – briefly illuminated flashes of phosphorescent memory that burn but a moment before they dim and dissipate. I swallow hard, fighting the urge to throw up. I feel nauseous. Sleepy. Still drunk. It's 6:47 a.m. and I'm due at work in exactly forty-three minutes.

Shit. I let the clock fall to the floor. Groan and pull the sheets up over my shoulder. I screw my eyes shut and will myself back to sleep, but I'm interrupted by a sharp knock.

"Oh, you're here," Rachel says, sailing through the door without waiting for a reply. "I didn't hear you come home last night. I thought you stayed at Ilena's."

"Jesus," I cry, clutching the sheet to my chest. "Don't you knock? I'm not even dressed."

"I knocked," she says. "You didn't answer. Besides, I'm not staying. I was just bringing up this junk you left downstairs." She tosses my box of photos on the bed. "If you're going to bring this flea market stuff into the house, keep it in your room, okay? Who knows where it's been." Rachel hates when I leave things in the common areas – also known as *her* turf. I've come home on more than one occasion to find neatly folded piles of my belongings on my bed. It infuriates me – the tiny tombstones serving as testament to the fact I don't actually belong here.

"Fine," I reply. "Now get out!"

"Shouldn't you be up by now?" Rachel asks. "You have to work, don't you?"

"I *am* up," I reply. "Look! I'm up, and I just want to get ready for work, so can you get out?"

"You look like shit," she says. She studies my face – takes in the chapped lips and smudged mascara, most of which has rubbed off on my pillow. "You can't go to work like that."

"For fuck's sake, Rachel – get out!" I reach for the first thing I can find. It turns out to be a teddy bear – a childhood keepsake that I've convinced myself I actually *do* keep just for the sake of it – despite the fact that I actually find it comforting at night, particularly when home alone. I hurl it in her direction, only half intending to hit my target. It glances off Rachel's right shoulder, and lands on the floor with an unsatisfying plushy *thump*.

"God, you can be such a little brat sometimes," she says, crossing her arms over her chest – completely unruffled. "If it weren't for me, you would have slept right through your alarm."

"Out!" I say, pointing towards the door.

"Fine," she says. "But don't forget about this afternoon."

"What about it?"

"This afternoon," she repeats. "You have to drive me to the airport."

Shit. It wasn't that I'd forgotten. I just hadn't remembered. That's all.

✧

I scrape myself off the sheets and brace my arm against the wall, fumbling towards the doorway. I trip over a pile of dirty laundry, and spy my purse perched on top – a black patent leather peak in a sea of white cotton socks. I pick it up, hoping it might contain some clue as to where I'd been – what I'd done or how I'd gotten home – some scant crumb of remembrance to fill in the blanks. To brush aside the dark curtain. The last thing I can recall is leaning up against Ilena on the dance floor. Sharing champagne and shouting over the bass.

I burrow through its contents but find nothing noteworthy. Keys. Cell phone. Some ID. Tossing it back on the floor, I catch my reflection in the full-length mirror. *Rachel was right*. I look only slightly better than I feel – pale and muslin-skinned, deeply pitted with shadowy hollows – a too thin canvas stretched over a too tall frame. I straighten my shoulders. Suck in my stomach. Stick out my chin.

I make a point not to linger too long in front of the mirror – never more than a cursory glance on my way out the door. It's a habit I've acquired after years of hoping to find someone else staring back. Years of being disappointed when I don't. This morning, as always, she's still there – *that* girl. Her hair running in rivulets down either side of her face – snarled skeins of caramel-coloured seaweed that wash over the fleshy promontories of her breasts.

I hate these. My breasts. They're uneven – asymmetrical – the right slightly larger than the left. It's always been this way. Ever since I was fourteen and the bee-stung buds of my nipples first promised to protrude. They never quite rose to what I imagined to be their full potential; and, in recent years, I'd come to think of them as my fraternally twinned peaks, separated at puberty, one genetically pre-destined to rise to greater heights than the other. My mother's always told me this is fairly typical; but somehow, her words have always failed to reassure me.

Glancing even further down, I spy my stomach. *I hate this too*. Hate the hint of slightly bowed flesh that bridges the expanse of my hips – as though independent of my body, not anchored to the other parts of me but merely held in place by the tension of my skin. I run my hand over it now, halting just above the untrimmed triangle of hair in the joint between my thighs. *No time for that today*, I tell the girl in the mirror. *You're going to be late.*

CHAPTER FIVE

"Hello," I call, "anyone home?" I inch through the door so as not to disturb the bell. Try to be discreet. A few lazy licks of reggae sift through the wall-mounted speakers, and a pungent yeasty aroma drifts out from the café's kitchen. Eli must already be here.

"Grace, is that you?" The sound of his voice sets my heart pounding and sends another wave of nausea rippling through my intestines. I slip behind the register and stow my purse as the kitchen door swings open, squeaking on its ungreased hinges.

"Hey, Eli," I say, ready with a story and a smile. "How's it going? I was just –"

"Save it," he says, "I don't want to hear your excuses." He dusts his hands off on his hips, streaking his standard issue black tee and cargo fatigues with flour. He crosses his arms over his chest, and I turn away, knowing I won't be able to suppress the slightest hint of a smile. Sometimes, for all his toughness, Eli reminds me of nothing so much as a 1950s housewife, armed with his spatula and his self-righteous indignation. "You're late."

"Really?" I reply. "I could've sworn I was on time. You know how it is," I say, pointing to my naked wrist, "...no watch."

"It's...7:47," he says, consulting his own digital monstrosity. "Trust me, you're late."

"Okay, I get it," I reply. "I won't be late again. Not *once* – not all summer. Girl Scout's honour," I say, crossing my fingers contritely over my heart. "You'll see."

"Yeah, I've heard that before," he replies. "Just pass me a plate, will you?"

I reach under the counter and hand off a small porcelain dish. "Seriously," I say. "I'll do better, Eli. I promise."

He takes the dish and heads towards the kitchen. "For your breakfast," he replies, holding it aloft. "Oh, and Grace," he says, smiling over his shoulder, "you better put a fresh pot of coffee on. Looks like you could use it."

"Thanks, *Dad*!" I call after him. I laugh and feel some of the morning's weight lift from my shoulders. Some balance restored. I can always count on Eli to let me off the hook. I pull an apron off the peg on the wall and sling it around my neck. The white noose will be my uniform for the next eight hours.

Weekday mornings my first order of business is to chalk the specials up on the board behind the register, and this is precisely what I'm doing at the exact moment that it happens – seasons change – and spring slides imperceptibly into summer.

"I'll be right with you," I call, responding to the bell's chime. "Hang on a second." I'm perched atop a folding metal stool attempting to punctuate a chalky white *i*. A stray hair tickles the end of my nose and the air conditioner hums overhead. It's early and the café is empty, save a host of dust motes dancing in the morning sun and the lone customer who's just walked in. "Sorry about that," I say, climbing down. "What can I get for you?"

Across the counter, a man fishes in his back pocket, presumably looking for his wallet. "No worries," he replies, not bothering to look up. "I thought I had some cash here..."

"It's okay," I say. "We take debit or credit too."

"But I could've sworn..." He stops sifting through a handful of change and glances up. "Hey, it's you," he says. "Gay bar girl!"

Stunned, I say nothing, my mind switching into overdrive as I try to place his face.

"I'm sorry," he laughs. "I only meant – well, what I meant to say is, you're the girl from last night – the one with the world's worst gay-dar."

I take a deep breath and allow the information to sink in. Permit an image to float to the surface of my subconscious. I have a vague recollection of a conversation shared with someone who looked like the man I see before me, but it remains fuzzy and indistinct. "Right," I reply, a hot flush of humiliation colouring my cheeks. "Of course."

"Well, without the disco ball, I'm sure I look quite different," he says. He smiles and pushes a pair of sunglasses up into his hair, closely cropped and dark – dusted with the salt-and-pepper signs of age. "What are you doing here?"

"What do you mean?" I ask, feeling suddenly trapped. Panicky. "I work here. What are you doing here?"

"Starbucks is closed," he says. "Renovations or something. I live just down the street."

"I see," I reply. "Well, small world."

"Have you worked here long?" he asks. "I'm surprised I've never seen you in the neighbourhood."

"No," I reply. "Well, yes – but only summers." I stare down at my apron, smoothing it straight over my shapeless hips. Without my make-up and my dress – my feminine accoutrements – I'm painfully aware of my unimpressive appearance.

"Do you live around here?" he asks, stepping back slightly, settling into the conversation. He slips his hands into the pockets of his jeans, performing this simple gesture with the same ease with which he wears his clothes – a periwinkle blue V-neck sweater, sleeves pushed up at the elbows – the casually indifferent attire of someone who has nowhere better to be on a weekday morning. *Probably cashmere.* Cashmere is the only kind of softness you can trust – the kind you can see before you can touch.

"Well, maybe you just never noticed me," I reply. "Before last night, I mean."

"Maybe," he says, "but I'm noticing you now."

The fabric beneath my arms grows damp with nervous perspiration and my heart beats rabbit-fast in my chest. I try to think of a suitably flirtatious response, but come up empty-handed, cowed in the face of his obvious charm. "So," I reply, "what can I get you?"

"You have something – right *there*," he says, gesturing towards my face, "on your cheek."

"What?"

"Something white," he says, "on your cheek." He leans forward as if to wipe it off. I brace myself and pull back sharply.

"Thanks," I reply. "I can do it." I pass the back of my arm across my face, removing the fine white powder that clings tenuously to the almost imperceptible layer of down just below my right eye. "So, what can I get for you?" I repeat. It's the third time that I've asked, and the question's dry utilitarian nature seems to break the spell – capture his attention.

"I'll take an Espresso Macchiato," he says. "To go, please." He slides a credit card from his wallet. "I'm sorry. I don't have any cash on me," he says, patting himself down. "Just change."

"It's fine," I reply. I punch the total into the machine and swipe his card. "Here you go." I tear the receipt tape off and hand it back to him with a pen. Cut a sidelong glance at him as he bends down to sign. The light of day reveals our age difference more plainly than it had the night before. The long deeply etched laugh lines. The neat little nests of crow's feet around his eyes. *Yes, he is old*; and yet, he doesn't look it – does not look aged.

Looking up, he catches me staring and smiles. I duck out of sight beneath the counter, pulling a milk carton from the fridge and measuring its contents into a stainless steel jug. I stab at the button to activate the steam wand, and am grateful for the temporary respite, but it doesn't last long. Not more than a minute.

"So, you work here full-time?"

"Like I said, only during the summer," I reply. "I'm a student. Well, I *was* a student. I just graduated."

I still haven't gotten used to the truth of these words. Still haven't gotten used to the thought of freedom. No new semester. No reassuring weight of days fixed out for me in a schedule of classes. No commitments. Only choices.

"Which university?" he asks. "UBC?"

I nod.

"Aha," he says, "a fellow alumnus."

"Pardon me?"

"I went there too," he replies. "Although that was a couple of years ago now."

"What did you study?"

"Law."

"Are you a lawyer?" I ask, beginning to regain my confidence. *My father is a lawyer.* Finally, something I know something about.

"I am," he says. "I'm working for myself right now though. A private deal for a friend. He's taking a company public and I'm helping him put the whole thing together. It's in Europe," he says. "Marseilles." I feign a knowing look, despite the fact that I have absolutely no idea what this means or where Marseilles is. It sounds French. Like somewhere my dad would send a postcard from. "What about you?" he asks. "What'd you study?"

"Not law," I reply, "that's for sure."

"You're not exactly forthcoming, are you?"

I focus intently on the dial of the thermometer, watching the needle's ascent from black to red. He waits, and I wonder whether he actually cares or not. Wonder, *Why me?* I search his face for a trace of genuine interest, but can't read him. He's a contradiction – gentle and courteous, but also probing and indiscreet.

"Art history," I reply. "I studied art history."

"That sounds pretty interesting," he says. "Like painters and stuff?"

"Yeah, something like that."

"What made you choose art history?" he asks. "I mean, what do you do with a degree like that?"

I smile, mostly to myself. This is a question I hear a lot, although usually from my mother. She wanted me to study science or medicine – something "real." Rational. Practical. Like her. Like Rachel. "I'm not sure yet," I reply. "I'm thinking about doing my Masters, of course – I mean, most people do. So I probably will." I like this lie. It sounds good. Believable even. Laden with intent. "Anyway, when I decide, I'll be sure to let both you *and* my mother know."

"I'm sorry," he says. "I didn't mean to pry – just curious."

"It's fine," I reply, "call it a sensitive subject. Besides, if my most intimate relations aren't privy to my life plans, it hardly seems fair that a total stranger should be. You haven't even told me your name."

"That's right," he says. "I never introduced myself." He thrusts a hand across the counter. "Jonathan Lewis, but everyone just calls me Jack."

"I know," I reply before I can catch myself. "I saw it on your credit card."

"Impressive," he says, smiling. I laugh despite myself – the first one I've let slip since we started talking. I can't help it. His smile is infectious – loose and easy – limber with use. "But why bother letting me tell you if you already know the answer?"

"Test of moral fibre," I reply. "Just to be sure."

"So I pass?"

"I think so," I say, placing his drink on the bar.

"Well, in that case, what have I won?"

"Pardon?"

"My prize," he repeats, "what have I won? You know, you still owe me that drink. Why don't you have a coffee with me some time?"

"I...I don't think so," I reply. I busy myself with the dials of the espresso machine. Shoot a jet of steam out of the wand and wipe it down with a damp cloth.

"Why not?" he asks. "Because if your hands are tied by a *No Dating the Customers* policy, I could easily acquire a taste for the coffee up the street."

"No, it's not that," I say. "It's just...I don't do that."

"Don't do what?"

"Date," I reply. "I don't date."

"Oh," he says, "Well, I guess I can't argue with that. But how about your name? Or is that under lock and key too?"

What does a trustworthy person look like? I consider this a moment as I study his face, his intentions still unclear – eclipsed by a thin veneer of charm. "It's Grace," I say, " Grace Linde."

"Well, Grace Linde...just in case you decide you do – date that is..." He grabs a cardboard cup holder and plucks a felt tip pen off the top of the espresso machine. Scrawls something on the back, places it face down and slides it towards me. "It's your call."

CHAPTER SIX

I slip the key in the lock, but the door's already open. I'm surprised to see Rachel sitting at the kitchen table, her dark brows lowered in obvious displeasure. Her legs are crossed, and one foot twitches in time to her impatience.

"Where've you been?" she demands. "You're an hour late."

Shit. Rachel. Airport. Toronto.

"How could you forget?"

"I didn't," I reply. "I just –." I sift through my standard bank of excuses, searching for something suitable. Something better than the truth, but it comes out anyway. "It just slipped my mind. Why didn't you remind me?"

"I did! And I called your phone about a million times."

"I didn't hear it," I reply. "It must be on silent."

"Forget it," she snaps back. "I gave up on you about half an hour ago – called a cab." She rakes her hands through her hair and consults her watch. "God, this is a fucking disaster, Grace. I'll be lucky if I even make my flight."

"My bad, okay?" I reply, making a beeline for my room. "It won't happen again."

"This is really important," she says, jumping up from her chair. "Why is that so hard for you to understand? This is *real* life – not the fucking coffee shop. I have a lot riding on this."

"Jesus, here we go," I reply, rolling my eyes. "I said I'm sorry. Just drop it, okay?"

"No, you didn't."

"What?"

"You didn't say you're sorry," she replies. "You *never* do."

"Seriously, Rachel?" I ask. "Give it a rest. I'm exhausted."

"All you care about is yourself, Grace," she says. "After all I've done for you, you can't even do this one simple thing for me. Can't you see how much this means?"

"You think I don't know how important this trip is?" I ask. "I get it, Rachel. It means you can finally leave Vancouver – leave the family – just like you've wanted to all along."

"You honestly think that's what this is about?" she asks. "You?"

"Please, Rachel. Don't you think it's pretty convenient that you get to go to Toronto while I'm stuck here with Mom? I mean, what am I supposed to do?"

"She's your mom too," Rachel replies. "I can't do everything myself."

"You're the one leaving!"

"And I'm the one that's been here all along," she says. "Who do think has been carrying you all this time, Grace. You have responsibilities too, you know. Maybe it's time you looked after them and stopped acting like such a child for a change. You're twenty-two now. I can't build my life around being your babysitter, not anymore."

I want to scream at her, but my lungs collapse like a compressed accordion. I feel the tears welling up behind my eyes, but I don't want to dignify her words with their due.

"You knew that this day was going to come, Grace," she says. "I told you, once you finished school you'd have to start supporting yourself."

"Oh, fuck you, Rachel. I don't *have* to live here," I reply. "I'm the one paying *your* mortgage. I can go anywhere. I can do whatever I want."

"Sure, Grace. Whatever," she says. "And don't forget, it's Mom that pays me. Not you. Besides, if I get this job, it won't matter anymore, will it?"

"Nope," I reply, "guess not."

Outside, a car horn honks.

"That'll be my cab," she says. "Look, I don't know when I'll be back – maybe a week or two – depending on what happens." She shoulders her bag and grabs a set of keys off the table. "Do me a favour, Grace? Take this time to make a plan. Get yourself sorted out. I know you just graduated, but life goes on. *Real* life. The sooner you accept that, the easier it'll be."

"Go," I say. "You'll miss your flight."

"Right," she replies. She moves to leave, but turns back. "Oh, and one more thing," she says. "Don't touch my car while I'm gone, Grace. And don't forget you're taking Mom to that concert on Saturday. I left the tickets in the front hall."

"I know," I reply. "You already told me."

"Yeah, well…it never hurts to have a reminder," she says. She turns and heads down the hall, the distance between our bodies growing greater. I watch the thread that's connected our lives for the past four years pull itself taut. Snap. Break. I hear the front door close. From now on, I know that everything will be different, but don't yet know how. I only know that we do not say good-bye; and, for us, this is a first.

I unbutton my jeans and slide them down my thighs, my hands still shaking from conflict and caffeine. They tangle in a web on the floor, and I kick them off one foot while stepping on them with the other. Torque myself into an unnatural pretzel to unhook my bra, letting it fall to the floor. I rub my shoulders, running my fingers over the faint indentations left in its wake. I stand naked on the bathroom floor, and listen to the sound of running water.

I love baths. Always have. When I was little, it was the only time I saw my mother. She took a bath every night before bed. Folding her frame into the tub, she'd close her eyes and sink beneath the surface. Re-emerge. Lean back. Her breasts bobbing now above, and now below the water. I was allowed to sit on the edge of the toilet and watch, so long as I was neither seen nor heard. It was her time.

She shaved her legs every single night. She'd sit up, reach for my father's can of Gillette and cup her palm, filling it with a softly whipped mound of cream. Slather it over her leg, now extended, a single pointed toe resting lightly on the cold water tap. She used my dad's plastic disposable razor – slicing a swath of pink flesh through the peaks of foam. In her hands, those articles looked transformed, and I remember thinking they'd never know such happiness against the stubbly flesh of my father's face. I remember thinking, *It must be good to be a woman.*

I spin the taps closed and lower myself into the tub, hovering on the brink of submersion, propping myself up on half-bent elbows that shake with exertion. The water is hot, *too* hot, but my body eventually adjusts and I'm able to slide beneath the surface. A rogue wave spills over the edge, splashing out over the black and white tiles, spreading quickly to my sponge-like clothes. *I'm making a mess.* I should care, but I don't. This is merely one of the great things about Rachel being gone.

Another is the privacy. With Rachel around, I'm not even safe behind a locked door. I suppose I wouldn't mind so much if masturbation weren't my foremost means of sexual gratification. But it is, and I do. I need the solitude. The silence and the quiet. The time and space to slip into both the mood and myself. Ordinarily, it doesn't take much. I keep it simple – just my hand – the pressure of my body exerted back on itself. I like this unadulterated connection – free from the complicating influence of electronic devices.

Tonight, I begin as I always do – by touching my bones. Caressing them with a hand so subtle it's barely conscious of its aim. *I like my bones.* They have good structure – barely there – inconspicuously bowed beneath the surface of my skin. And yet, they're sound – avian-like in their blend of form and function. They make me feel light and breakable at the same time that I feel strong and capable, able to inflict pleasure but also pain.

I slip my hands into the water and cross my arms over my chest, seamlessly slotting my fingers into the dips and valleys of my body's ribbed cage. I run the ridge of my clavicle, stroking the camber of its curve, picking up the subtle hum of my body's tune. Reaching down, I close my eyes and slide inside myself, allowing my fingers to find a foothold in my folds. I'm well-versed in my own mechanics, and try to relax into the ritual. Wait for the release. Brace myself in anticipation of the crescendo before climax. But tonight, something doesn't satisfy. There is no click – no steady climb. *Something is wanting.* Something I can't find within myself.

With a frustrated sigh, I snap my eyes open and leave off my ministrations. Sitting up, I pull myself to my full height and splash water over the floor as I do. As I step from the tub, it pools in an impudent puddle at my feet. I sweep my toe through it in a long lazy arc, wrapping a towel around my torso and tracing an angel wing of water with my foot.

I think of Rachel and her wrath. Think of how I don't give a damn. Leave the room. Leave the light on. Leave the wing forgotten on the floor.

CHAPTER SEVEN

The moon lights the way across my room, but not light enough. Squinting in the dark, I stub my toe on the latest addition to my collection – the box of photos I haven't had time to explore let alone sort. I stoop down to pick it up, moving towards the window, box in tow. My wet hair lies in wilted hanks down my back, and the cool night air goose pimples the flesh stretched across my chest. I wrap my towel even tighter and perch on the wooden ledge, set the box in my lap, and dangle one leg over the sill, dragging a toe along the sandpapery shingles of the roof. I flip through the photos, sifting through my feelings and the feelings that I see.

A raucous-looking family dinner with beer steins and sloppy smiles. *Happiness*. A pig-tailed girl in knee socks, arms about the neck of a man with a softly greyed muzzle. *Affection*. And then, my mystery woman, the image of her partially obscured face returning to haunt me here in my room. I pull the picture out and angle it towards the moon. Scrutinize it more closely.

Decide to write her story. I do this often – amuse myself by playing with the lives of the people in my photos. I give them fictitious names and families and friends, places to belong to and things that belong to them. Tonight, I try to do this with her – carve out a narrative for her anonymity – but I can't seem to pin her down. I close my eyes, attempting to slip into character.

A few blocks away, the wind blows gently from the beach, a slight sea breeze that frosts the inside of my lungs with a fine crust of salt. This helps. Suddenly, it's my hair that blows before my face – tickling my nose. My toes that curl, cashew-like, around the grains of sand. I'm the one that raises my hand and peers out towards the horizon.

I open my eyes. Gaze over the crenulated crests of the treetops; and, for the first time that day, I think of Jack. I think of him, and wonder where he is – what he's doing. Marseilles. *What would it be like to go with him?* Maybe he could take me – away from this place – on a plane, a train...a yacht. *Arm candy...a professional lady of leisure.* I like the thought. To go somewhere else – somewhere I could send postcards from – raggedy edged corners of a world they've never seen. All of them. My dad. My mom. Rachel. I run my finger over her half-turned face, half-expecting to feel my own, or at least to feel her warmth. She looks so vital – so alive – even in black and white. *Where will I put her? My mystery woman.*

I rise from the window and turn towards my shelves. Scan the labels, but none seem quite right. I want to say Anticipation, but this is wrong. I know that she's not just waiting for something, she's wishing for it. And so, I say Desire – say it before I even realize I haven't got a spot for this feeling. I glance around for a stray box, but see nothing suitable, just an elongated square of moonlight that catches my eye – casts an inverse shadow on the floor beside my bed. And there, peeking out from my purse, I spy it – the cup holder – Jack's name barely visible by the light of the moon.

"Grace!" he calls, extending an arm above his head. Jack stands directly in front of the café, leaning up against a car, a pair of dark sunglasses obscuring his eyes. I wave and make my way towards him, my stomach twisting itself even tighter into the knot I've been nursing all day.

51

He looks better than I remembered – shorts and a black tee with some indecipherable white graffiti sprayed across the front. In my faded jeans and T-shirt, I feel suddenly sloppy and self-conscious.

"Well, hello there," he smiles. He leans down to plant a friendly double-barrelled European kiss on my cheek. The gesture takes me by surprise and I pull back awkwardly, leaning in again too soon, attempting to rectify my error. He graciously ignores my lack of grace. "And so, we meet again."

"We do," I reply.

"I'm glad you called."

"Yeah...well, I thought you deserved that consolation prize after all," I reply. "For the champagne at least..."

"Well, you look great," he replies, giving me a quick once over.

"I meant the coffee," I say, blushing. "And I can assure you, I don't." I throw my arms wide and survey my coffee-stained state. Smooth back a few stray hairs that have escaped my bun. "Are you sure I shouldn't go home and change?"

"You're just right," he replies. "Trust me."

He's lying, but I like the compliment; and my cheeks glow warmly with the summer sun and a false sense of self-confidence. "So, which way?" I ask, glancing down the sidewalk. "You were very vague on the phone."

"Aha," he replies, "that...is a secret." He reaches behind him and into the open window of the car. Evidently, the inconspicuous black Toyota is his, and I'm surprised. I get the sense that he's got money to spare, and I'd been expecting something grander – flashier. But, if anything, I think it makes me like him more. I would never have felt comfortable getting into something like a Porsche. I can do a Prius.

Jack produces something from the passenger seat, unfurling a thin strip of fabric – purple with slivers of silver.

"A tie?" I ask. Curious. Confused. Hesitant. "What's that for?"

"It's not just a tie," he says. "It's a blindfold."

I laugh, but it subsides to an uncertain chuckle as I see that he's in earnest. "You're kidding, right?"

"Nope."

"But, I'm not putting that on."

"Sure you are," he says. "Come here." He beckons me forward, but I stay put – frozen with incredulity. I've never been blindfolded before, and have relegated it to my *Not To Do List* along with being spoon-fed in public. It's not my style; and yet, I admit I'm beginning to enjoy myself a little – the attention at least. I'm aware of passersby glancing in our direction, studying us from afar – two tentative bodies turned towards each other. Part of me wants to give in – fall into the dark with him. But part of me says I should keep some semblance of control.

"I can't," I reply. "Really. I mean, I hardly know you."

"So?" he asks, shrugging his shoulders.

"So?" I repeat. "How do I know you won't kidnap me and sell me into white slavery or something?"

"Well," he says, "I guess you'll just have to trust me."

I glance down the sidewalk in either direction, not sure what type of salvation I'm hoping for. I'm fresh out of excuses, but I don't want to be a spoil sport. Prudish. Stuffy. He's supposed to be the old-fashioned one. The *old* one. I'm supposed to be young – fun and sexy and spontaneous. I hate the thought of giving in, but I hate the thought of disappointing even more.

"Okay," I say, "fine. You win."

"Perfect," he says. "Allow me." He takes the tie and clasps my shoulders, spinning me around. His hands brush past my ears as he brings it over my brow, knotting it firmly at the base of my bun. He adjusts the fabric, sliding it down the bridge of my nose; and, suddenly, brightness turns to black, blotting out the summer sun. As I'm plunged into darkness, I feel slightly panicky, acutely aware of the tension in my stomach. I swallow hard. Clench my fists slightly. Feel sweat beginning to bead up on my palms.

"Okay," he says. "Now, give me your hand."

I hold out my arm and he guides me towards the car, opens the door and helps me find the passenger seat. I lower myself with an uncertain *thud*, and he helps me tuck my legs into the car. Slams the door. A few seconds later, the other opens on the driver's side, and an arm grazes my chest as my seatbelt glides across it. "So," he says, "are you ready?"

The ride passes rather quickly and I'm thankful. Jack has taken the opportunity to pepper me with questions and the pressure in my chest is beginning to build. I've never been interrogated with a blindfold on before and it feels precisely like being caught in the crosshairs of an executioner without knowing where they stand. It's difficult to be coy in this situation – let alone concentrate on the task at hand. Everything comes out sounding flat and dull and matter-of-fact, as though I'm trying to pass a lie detector test – keep my pulse even and my heart from racing.

"*Et voila*," he says, "here we are." Keys jingle in the ignition, and the engine dies away. I can hear the click of a seatbelt – first his, then mine – the release of pressure over my lap as he allows it to retract. He's gentle – careful not to let the belt hit my shoulder or my chin.

Thank God. I feel slightly nauseous, not from the motion, but from the metallic tang of air conditioned air on the back of my tongue. I haven't asked where we're going, and he hasn't offered to tell me. "Can I look now?"

"Not yet!" he says. The car door slams and a set of feet jog around behind me. To my right, the door swings open, and fresh air hits me square in the face. "Give me your hand," he orders. "Watch your head."

I offer my arm to my invisible footman – feel foolish in my blindness but trust that my feet will find the ground. That he will help me if they don't. I stand and a set of hands grasps my shoulders. Spin me around. His fingers work the knot as the fabric falls away. Squinting, I allow my eyes to adjust to the early evening sun. Survey my surroundings.

"Seriously?" I ask. "Are we really here?"

"Seriously," he says with a smile.

I recognize the familiar orange lettering at once – a word I've known well my whole life, but feel like I'm now seeing for the first time – perhaps because I'm seeing it as an adult and not a child. PLAYLAND.

CHAPTER EIGHT

We stand in a parking lot off Hastings Street – right in front of Playland, a local amusement park. I used to come here with my father as a child. My mother never joined us. She isn't fond of rides. She says she likes to keep her feet firmly planted on the ground.

"I thought it'd be fun," he replies. "Have you ever been on The Coaster?"

"Of course," I say, confident at least in this. The Coaster is a Vancouver institution, a sprawling network of nearly seventy-foot drops. It's renowned for its wooden structure – unique. They don't make them like that anymore. Too dangerous. Personally, I agree. I've never taken much pleasure in the experience, but it's the only ride my dad would ever go on. He said it gave him a kick – the potent cocktail of excitement and fear. It usually just made me feel sick.

"Well, let's go," Jack says, holding out his hand. I don't take it – slip mine into my pockets instead. I've never held hands with a man before, not unless you count my father; and though Jack may only be slightly younger, it's not the same. Not the same at all.

"So," he says, "are you scared?"

"No," I lie, as we snake our way through the turnstile. I can hear the shrieks of the ride's other victims – cries of either dread or delight – difficult to discern.

"Good," he says, "because we're next." We stand on the wooden platform, separated from the track by a single set of riders. Soon, they too are handed into a waiting car and swept out of the station. It disappears around a curved arm of rails, trundling towards the first hill. The second train pulls in and we step back to allow the passengers to disembark – two teenage boys in T-shirts and baggy jeans, their faces flushed with fear and exhilaration. They hold baseball caps in their hands, and sheepishly slide them over their windswept hair.

"After you," Jack says. I settle myself onto the vinyl seat, temporarily mended with duct tape, and Jack squeezes in beside me. Limbs akimbo, we try to adjust ourselves. I look for a seat belt but there isn't one. Jack sees me scrambling and wraps an arm around my shoulders. Its weight feels good across my back. Better than a seat belt. Stronger. Safer.

The attendant lowers the bar over our laps and gives it a few rough jerks, testing its soundness. "Purse stays here," he says, pointing to a sign. *No loose objects.*

I hand it to him and he tosses it on the platform, finishes checking the cars and returns to his podium. He punches at the panel in front of him. A harsh metallic trill rings out overhead and the train jumps to life. The tick and whirr of a chain humming beneath our feet as we sail smoothly around the first bend.

It's just beginning to grow dark and the lights of the fairgrounds fly by – a flurry of neon-infused colour. We climb the first hill and I watch the earth disappear at an odd forty-five degree angle. I briefly consider how much I'm trusting to science and to fate, a pair of rather strange bedfellows. I sit perfectly still – poker-straight. Beside me, Jack stirs.

"No hands," he says, gesturing to my white-knuckle grip on the bar. "It's better that way – a bigger rush."

I nod, but ignore him, tightening my throttle-hold on the bar. We crest the hill and the mechanical strain falls away. I can see the zigzag expanse of the North Shore Mountains – indigo blue on the black horizon – skating over the surface of the water. *Here we are.* Suspended in space and time – caught in the in-between – sea and sky, daylight and dusk, flying and falling. I only have an instant for this thought, the time it takes to draw a single breath. *In. Out.* And then, an imperceptible hand takes hold. The balance tips, and the subtlety of science urges us on – seventy feet at seventy-five miles per hour.

I scream. We both do. I scream until there's nothing left, and nothing left to do but laugh. Laugh until I cry. Cries that die in the same breath that bears them from my lips, drowned in the rattle and roar of metal on wood. We hit the bottom and swing seamlessly into the next ascent – safe – at least, for now. I lower my arms, realizing then that I had in fact let go. Beside me, Jack just smiles – lowers his arms – squeezes my shoulder.

"Where to now?" Jack asks. "What next?" It's officially evening, and the grounds boast a technicolour rainbow that dances feverishly over every surface. "What do you want to do?"

I hesitate. Unsure. I've only ever been here as a daughter. Don't know how to navigate it as a date; and yet, I have plenty of people to model myself after. There are always a lot of couples here. It's a good place to look like one – swing hammers and win oversized stuffed toys – laugh and be admired.

"I don't know," I reply. "It's up to you."

"I have an idea," he says. "It'll be fun. You up for a game?"

"That depends," I reply. "What kind?"

"Mini golf," he says. "I have a sneaking suspicion I can kick your butt."

"What makes you so sure?" I ask. "For all you know, I could be a pro."

He smiles. His eyes meet mine and I quickly look away, attempting to break their persuasive pull, pondering his request. My mouth is dry and my tongue lies like fruit leather against the back of my teeth. The air tastes sweet and salty – like popcorn and perspiration.

"Come on," he says. Without warning, he grabs my hand. He grabs my hand and I let him. Feel my stomach thrill at the sensation of his fingers finding mine, giving me the courage to defy the glances we draw. A man. A woman. *A girl.* I cannot blame them. Nor can I care. *Let them stare. They could never understand.* "This way," he says, "follow me."

CHAPTER NINE

My phone rings. *Wake up*, it says; but I'm tired – exhausted. It rings again and I reach out to feel around on the nightstand, my fingers closing over the cool plastic. *Got it*. And it's her. I know it before I can even say *Hello*.

"Grace?" she asks. "Is that you?"

"Hi, Mom."

"Are you still asleep?"

"It's 6:30." Much like Rachel, my mother's always been an early riser. If she's up, she just assumes the rest of the world is too.

"I realize that, Grace," she says. "But I wanted to catch you before work."

"Anyway, I'm awake now," I reply. "What's up?"

"Saturday," she says. "The concert starts at 8:00, so I'll pick you up at quarter after 7:00."

"That's okay," I say. *Typical*. Just like Rachel. Never asks. Only tells. "I don't need a ride. I'll just meet you there."

"Fine," she replies. "Suit yourself, but please don't be late. You have the tickets."

"I'll be there, Mom," I say. "I've got to go, okay? I have to work."

✧

It's Friday. Last shift of the week, and the eight hours seem interminably long. I can't stop thinking about the previous evening. Can't stop thinking about Jack. On more than one occasion, I catch myself furtively fingering my clavicle – sliding my hand beneath the straps of my apron and into the V'd neck of my T-shirt. I know the hand is his, as is the gentle pressure of my palm on my chest.

"Daydreaming?" he asks. Startled, I stand at attention. I hadn't even heard the bell ring. I run my hands over my hair in a vain attempt to make myself presentable. Smooth my apron over my hips. "I thought I'd find you here."

"No, you didn't," I reply, regaining my composure, "you knew you would."

"Fine," he says. "I'm guilty, but what are you going to do? Charge me with buying coffee?"

"Is that why you're here?"

"That depends," he says. "Am I under oath?"

"No," I reply, "just your word."

"Well, in that case, I confess to owning an espresso machine," he says. "Does that answer your question?" I smile, and he takes it as an invitation to continue. "I just wanted to tell you again what a nice time I had last night."

"I did too," I reply. "Thanks."

"Don't mention it," he says. "I'm glad you changed your mind."

"About what?" I ask. "Dating?"

"No," he says, "about me."

I smile. Lower my eyes. Silent.

"Listen," he says, "I'm off to France to finish this deal on Sunday, but I'd like to see you again before I go."

"You're seeing me right now," I reply, still unsure as to what I want to happen. How far I want this to go.

"Is that a yes or a no?" he asks, unfazed by or unwilling to play games. He lays only two choices before me, coercing me into committing, one way or another.

"Yes," I say, before I can think too much. Before the offer can be taken off the table. "It's a yes."

"Great. I've got a friend's birthday party tonight," he says. "I know it's short notice, but are you free?"

"Sure," I reply, regretting it the moment I say it. I should've fabricated some plans – played hard to get – or at least hard*er*. "Are you sure it's okay? I mean, I haven't been invited. Would he mind?"

"Of course," he says. "And *he* is actually a she – the same woman I was with the other night – an old friend. You'll like her."

"Where is it?"

"Yaletown," he says. "Do you know the Opus Hotel? It's just in the lounge there."

"Of course," I say, nodding, in spite of my ignorance. I've heard the name before, but don't know where it is. I'll have to look it up. "What time should I meet you?"

"I have a better idea," he replies. "Why don't you come by my place before? We can have a quick drink on my patio. I have a great view of English Bay."

"Okay," I reply, "sure."

"Great," he says. "So, it's a date."

"Sounds good," I reply. *Why not?* Drinks at his house? *Just go with it*, I think. *Just let go.*

"Was that the repair guy?" Eli asks, stalking out from the kitchen. He surprises me, and my cheeks flush with frustration. *Hasn't he ever heard of knocking?* And then, I remember where I am. "Hello?" he says, "Earth to Grace. I asked you a question."

"What?"

"The air conditioner," he says, "it's broken. Was that the repair guy?"

"Oh...no," I reply. "It wasn't."

"Man, what is up with you today?" he asks, bending down low to adjust some sandwiches in the display case. "You're totally out of it."

"Sorry," I reply. "I guess I'm just a little tired." Jack hadn't dropped me off until midnight, and I'd lain awake until two. Unable to sleep. Unsatisfied and unable to satisfy myself.

"Hot date?" he asks.

"No," I lie. "Not exactly." I don't know why I don't tell Eli. Perhaps I know he wouldn't approve. Perhaps I know that no one will. I even have to wonder if I do, or if I care.

"Well, snap out of it," he says. "You're giving me the creeps." He disappears back into the kitchen, and I find myself alone again. It's quiet in the café, uncharacteristically so, and I rest my elbows on the counter. I lean towards the shaft of light that falls on the oak floor. Study it, searching for the telltale dance of dust, but without the gust of air, the specks just hang there – inert – immobile. They remind me of the boats in the Bay, their sails suddenly slackened, stranded on calm and glassy waters. Forsaken by the wind. Forgotten.

To me, the thought of languishing in the doldrums has always seemed a fate worse than death. I realize then, with crystal clarity, that Jack is the most exciting thing that's ever happened to me. This thought doesn't shock me, but it does scare me. *How much would I withstand to hold onto this moment?* I'm not sure yet. Just return to stroking my clavicle, moving my hand in a steady metronomic back and forth, just to know I can.

CHAPTER TEN

Sweat slips down the trough of my spine. I'm nervous. Late.
The address Jack gave is for Point Grey Road, a beachfront
property in the wealthier part of town. I go on foot, which
proves to be a mistake. It feels like crossing the boundary from
a tent city of squatters into the cloistered shrub-lined
sanctuaries of the elite. Gone are the soaring peaks of three-
storey porch-lined houses. Gone are the huddled masses of
stucco apartment blocks. In their place, a seemingly never-
ending row of purposefully idiosyncratic mini mansions, each
with its own security fence.

From my house, it's only a ten minute walk, but I haven't
accounted for how long it will take in four-inch heels. I cradle
a bottle of wine in my right arm – Sparkling Shiraz. I'd picked
it up after work from a local specialty shop, choosing it out of
ignorance and desperation and paying more than I could
afford. Now, it feels all wrong, the most obvious reason being
that it should be chilled. Condensation seeps through the paper
bag and dampens my dress, plastering it to my side.

This is it, I think, consulting the piece of paper, the ink
beginning to run from the heat of my hand. I push the buzzer
on the intercom beside the driveway. I wait. I wait for what
feels like forever, mostly because, standing there, with just

myself, I feel utterly foolish. As though I've walked up on foot to a drive-thru window. I wish then that I'd taken Rachel's car – that I weren't so damn afraid of her, even from afar.

He's already got the door open – watching as I stumble up the cobble-stone drive in my stilettos. He looks great. Cool. Relaxed. Jeans and a simple black button-up shirt, undone at the cuffs. "I'm glad you found the place," he says. "You didn't have any trouble?"

"No," I reply, attempting to look nonchalant, "I found it fine."

"You look amazing," he says. He draws me in for another of his European kisses; and, this time, I'm ready for him – give and receive it with something close to grace.

"Thank you," I reply, an intense wave of gratification washing over me. I've chosen wisely – a loose-fitting white sheath dress – sleeveless and unembellished with a simple boat neck collar. It hangs away from my body, lightly grazing the few curves I have. "Here," I say, forcing my offering on him. "I wasn't sure if you like white or red."

"I like everything," he replies. "Come on. Let's get this open." He shoos me inside and closes the door behind me. My eyes adjust to the dimly lit interior, taking in the slate-lined foyer and the sunken living room. The stone hearth and the artwork. Not just prints. *Actual* art. Scattered artefacts of an adult life. He ushers me down a darkened hall, and I follow close behind, cutting sidelong glances as I do, each room a picture of perfection – precisely like the perfectly placed hairs on the back of his neck.

"It's beautiful," I say. *You're beautiful.*

"Sorry if it's a bit of a mess," he replies. "I didn't know I'd be leaving again so soon. I just got back from vacation last week."

"Really?" I ask. "Where?"

"Thailand," he replies. "Have you ever been?"

"No, I haven't." I don't mention that I've never been anywhere. Never left the continent. The country. Just been to Toronto and back.

"Seriously?" he asks. "Then you have to see my photos. They're amazing. I just loaded them onto my computer." He places a hand on the small of my back and directs me to a room on the right. My dress presses against my skin, and I hope he can't feel my nervous perspiration.

"This is my study," he says, reaching around the corner to flip a switch. The walls are lined with books, most of which have the word *Law* somewhere in the title. A dark heavy-looking desk sits at the far end of the room, the blue screen of a computer beaming out at us. "This is where I try to get some work done," he says, "but it's been tough lately with all the travel."

"And that?" I ask, "Is that work too?" I point to an easel in the corner. It holds a half-finished still life, some yellow pears and a wine glass on a marbled tabletop.

"Oh, you might say that," he replies. He advances towards the painting, an unmistakable tone of pride in his voice. "I took a class last year. I try to keep it up," he says. "In my line of work, I don't get many opportunities to be creative. I'm always trying my hand at something new."

"What are you taking now?"

"Stand-up comedy," he says.

"Seriously?"

"Yeah, it's pretty fun actually – a lot of improvisation," he replies, "but I'm good at that – thinking on my feet." He smiles and winks at me. "After all, I'm a lawyer."

I turn to examine the rest of the room, and notice a glass case set on stilts shunted up against the wall. It looks like a pinball machine, but wider – without the carnivalesque bells and whistles. I move towards it, and I feel his gaze follow me.

"Ah," he says, "*mes papillons*." I shoot him a quizzical look and he provides a translation for my benefit. "My butterflies."

"Butterflies," I repeat. *Butterflies*. I lay my hand on the edge of the glass, transfixed by the kaleidoscopic effect of the rainbow-winged specimens. "You collect butterflies?"

"Yes," he says, "or rather, I inherited the collection from my father. He was a botanist, but he collected insects on the side. He had a beetle collection too, but I didn't keep that one. Threw it out. But these...they were so beautiful. I didn't have the heart."

"How did he get so many?" I ask. "Isn't it hard to catch a butterfly?"

"No, not if it's done properly."

"How?" I ask. "With a net or something?"

"Sort of," he says. "That's a common misconception. Nets are only used for the first part. Once they're captured, most collectors just use a killing jar."

"A *killing* jar?" I repeat. "What's that? It sounds awful."

"Sounds worse than it really is," he says. "It's just a glass jar filled with ether. It knocks them out before they can hurt themselves trying to escape."

"That's terrible," I reply. "Isn't there some other way?"

"Well, you can kill them by hand," he says. "But that means you have to crush their thorax. Like this," he says. Reaching down, he makes a pinching gesture with his thumb and two fingers, tweezing my skin between them. "It works," he says, "but it ruins the specimen. Look. See here..." He points to an orange and black butterfly near the bottom of the case. The slender body betrays a slight bend, so subtle you wouldn't see it unless you sought it out. "The ether is quicker and leaves no trace."

"It seems like a strange hobby," I say. "Cruel even."

"True, but it's also an art form," he says. "Death is just part of the process. Besides, they don't suffer – not long anyway."

"But aren't most hobbies supposed to be casualty-free?"

"Not at all. People die all the time pursuing their passions," he says. "Climb mountains. Ride rapids. Skydive. It just depends on the person...and the passion."

"But that's different," I reply, crossing my arms over my waist. "People are capable of choosing. These butterflies...they didn't have that chance."

He considers this a moment, both of us gazing down into the matching sets of dashed and dotted wings. "Anyway," he says, "you have to admit, they're beautiful, aren't they?"

"Yes," I reply. "Yes, they are." At the same time, I can't help but wonder if the brutality is worth it. To be admired for nothing more than beauty's sake. *Does the end really justify the means?* We both fall silent and he slips his hand into his pockets – shifts his weight first to one foot, and then the other. "Well, what about you?" he asks. "What are some of your hobbies?"

"Just the usual," I reply, turning away from the case. "Reading. Writing. Photography."

"You're a photographer?"

"No," I reply, "a collector."

"A collector?" he asks. "What do you mean?"

"I collect old photographs," I reply. "From second-hand shops. Flea markets. Anyplace."

"Pictures of strangers?" he asks. "But, what for? I mean, why?"

"Because," I say, still unsure if I can trust him with the long answer. "Just because."

"*Because?*" he repeats. "That's all I get? Come on, you must have a better reason than that. No one collects something for no reason."

"Fair enough," I reply. "I guess you're right. I just like saving what someone else has tossed away. Photos last forever, regardless of what happens. I like the endurance of their beauty," I say. "In fact, it's sort of like your butterflies, I guess – only no one had to die."

"Sure they did," Jack replies. "You just don't see it. I mean, what happens after?"

I don't know, I think. *And I don't care.* "Who knows," I reply, shrugging my shoulders. "It's just a collection, that's all."

"Right...well," he says, my curt response silencing him on the subject, "I think there's a sunset waiting for us somewhere out back. Shall we?"

"You were going to show me your pictures of Thailand," I remind him.

"Oh, yeah," he says, "I forgot, but another time. I promise." He ushers me out of the room and follows close behind, flipping the switch as we leave, softly shutting the door.

CHAPTER ELEVEN

"I have to be honest," he says, "I was a little surprised you accepted my invitation."

"Oh, why?"

"Well, most women – at least, most women I've dated – wouldn't agree to come to a man's house on a second date."

"Really?"

"Don't get me wrong," he says, "it's great. Women have far too many rules about dating; but then, something tells me you're different from most women."

I blush. Smile.

"What?" he asks. "Does that embarrass you?"

"No," I reply, "it's just that word. *Woman.*"

"What about it?"

"Nothing. It's just...exactly how old do you think I am?"

"Ah," he says, "we're playing that game now?"

"We have to eventually, don't we?"

"Fine," he says. "I'll go first. How old do you think *I* am?"

"I honestly don't know," I reply. This is the truth. I know that Jack's old – much older than me; but, when we're together, we seem to find a way to meet in the middle – halfway between his years of experience and the waning shadow of my youthful expectations. I like the sympathetic understanding inherent in our silence on the subject thus far, and I don't want to spoil it with speculation.

"I'm forty-five," he replies. "I'll be forty-six in August."

"Oh..." I say, trying not to betray my surprise. But I am – both by the number and by his candid response. I knew there was an age gap, but I hadn't realized it was nearly twenty-five years wide. I try not to flinch. "And what about me?" I ask. "How old do you think I am?"

"You," he says, with another wink, "are twenty-two."

"I am," I reply "How did you know that?"

"I didn't," he says. "But you mentioned that you just graduated. I took a lucky guess." He fills a glass with red wine and pushes it across the table, filling a second one for himself.

"Right," I say. *Of course*. I take the wine. Take a sip. Wonder why it seems that everyone but me can sound so self-assured when they take a shot in the dark. I envy it. I envy him; and, far from feeling superior in my youth, I admire him in his age.

"So, now that we've gotten that out of the way, can we enjoy this?" he asks, sweeping his arm wide to take in the sea, the sky and the slowly descending sun. "Best seat in the house," he says. "This is why I bought this house. This is what sold me."

I glance over my shoulder at the flat-roofed system of tiers and terraces. Glass and gunmetal grey. Wood and windows. It has a certain rustic modernity that lends its cool lines and hard edges a softness and familiarity – allows it to blend seamlessly into the sandy rock-lined shores of the West Coast. "How long have you been here?" I ask.

"Almost seven years now," he says. "And you?"

"Since I was eighteen."

"And you're happy here?" he asks. "In Kitsilano? You like it?"

"For the most part," I reply. "I might move. I mean – travel or something. I'm still not sure." It's the first time I've given voice to this thought, and I'm not certain whether it's true, or whether I only wish it were.

"God, I love travelling," he says. "Where will you go?"

"I don't know," I reply. "I'm not really sure. I mean, I've never thought about it before." I spin the stem of my wine glass, draining it and allowing him to fill it again. I take another sip, and feel the hinges of my tongue loosen ever so slightly. Feel the liquor working on the strength of my resolve. Feel myself opening and opening up. "When I was little, my sister, Rachel, she had this globe in her room. People don't really have them anymore I guess, but she had this globe, and she wouldn't let me touch it. I used to sneak into her room to look at it. I'd just sit there for hours and spin it. Close my eyes and let my finger fall," I say. "I was convinced I could open them again and find myself transported."

"Really?" he asks. "I love that. Did it ever work?"

"Yeah, right," I reply, "nothing so easy."

"So," he says. "Why not now? You're young. Graduated. You can do whatever you want. I'd kill to be twenty-two again. So fresh. So free. You have your whole life before you."

To be twenty-two, I think. *Can he even remember what that means?* I survey the experiential lines etched across his forehead – the insouciant weathered countenance of composure – and I feel a sudden pang of jealous anxiety. "Freedom?" I ask. "Falling from the sky into a foreign land...with no map? No compass? No *nothing*? You think that's being free? Some people would call that being lost."

"Yes," he says, "I think that's exactly what it means. I still remember that first trip – Australia. The first one I'd taken on my own – without my parents. No family...no friends...*yet*. That first step – it was the first freedom I'd really known – that any of us really know. That's what being twenty-two is all about."

"Yeah, but you can only say that because you're..." I stop myself then. Only think it instead. *Old.* "Hindsight is 20/20," I reply. "If you already know you can fly, then flying doesn't seem so scary, does it?"

"Do you always take yourself this seriously?" he asks, smiling. "Whatever happened to standard second-date questions like *What's your favourite book?* or *Do you prefer cats to dogs?*"

I laugh. Regret my scepticism, or at least that I haven't bothered to cover it up. And yet, with a few drinks inside me, I find I don't mind owning my inadequacies so much. Allowing my insecurities to show through the cracks. I can confess to my shortcomings because I'm beginning to feel that I'll surely measure up elsewhere. True, Jack has me beat when it comes to life lessons, but inexperience is a sin that youth more than makes up for in other ways. Sometimes, the thing itself is sufficient. To be young is to be enough.

"Fine," I say, "We'll do it your way. So, cats or dogs?"

"Cats," he says. "But I don't have one. I travel a lot. It's too much of a commitment."

"It's a pet," I reply, "not a person. I hate to think what would've happened to your kids."

"*Touché*," he says, laughing. "My would-be progeny has escaped thus far, but who knows – I might still reform – have some kids. I've always admired men who do – I like the idea."

"Well, the house is certainly big enough," I say. "For just one person? Don't you ever get lonely here by yourself?"

"No," he says matter-of-factly, "No, I don't." He leaves no shadow of doubt. No room for maybe. No ifs. No buts. "I like my solitude."

Suddenly, I understand what he's trying to tell me, and I realize what it means. A man doesn't get to be single at Jack's age unless he likes the life he leads. Unless by choice. It's undeniable – he's a catch, which carries certain privileges, but also certain prerequisites. It must take some doing to remain uncaught. Unattached. It must take some skill. But the reward is great. Jack's confirmed bachelorhood is made-to-order, called into being by desire, defying the very laws against which nature pits most men. At his age, he can still say, *What if,* with something like conviction. He can speak of having children at a time when most are past their parental prime only because he still sleeps with them – young girls, that is. Young women. Me.

Suddenly, I have an overwhelming urge to empty my bladder. I'd been holding it, as it seemed somehow unladylike to excuse myself, but I cannot wait anymore. "Would you mind telling me where the bathroom is?" I ask, pushing my chair from the table.

"I can do better than that," he replies, "I can show you." He steps behind me, guiding me towards the house. Our intertwined reflections rise to meet us in the window. Jack leans down low and whispers in my ear. "We make a good looking couple," he says, "don't you think?"

I nod in dozy drunken assent. *It's true*. He's beautiful, and I feel beautiful. And life with him feels exactly like looking at a picture of a girl who looks like me. I toss my head just so. Angle my body just so. Turn my face towards some imaginary light. A freshly minted leaf, drinking in the vital radiance of the summer sun. Light and light of heart. Carefree and careless.

When I return, Jack is nowhere to be found. I pad towards the edge of the patio, placing my wine glass on the low lying stone wall. I perch beside it, my heart fixed soundly in my throat, attempting to arrange my body to appear to its best advantage. I rake my fingers through my hair and smooth out some wrinkles on my dress. Pivot on the concrete ledge, and bring my legs up beside me in what I hope is an artful and unstudied manner. I lean back a little, supporting myself with one hand, and the rough rock face etches an impression in my palm. I try not to think about the pain. Relax. Breathe into the warm liquid sensation of the liquor.

"That is one of the sexiest things I've ever seen," Jack says, spotting me from the doorway, drinks in hand. I breathe. Brace myself to back the bold declaration. To deserve it. He sets the glasses on the table and approaches me. Touches my cheek. Lays a hand on my shoulder, as though to ask if I'll mind missing a party for a friend I've never met – a party which may or may not have been fictitious in the first place.

I lower my eyes, and bring my lips to the back of his hand. *No, I don't mind.* Don't care. He kisses me then, cupping his hands about my face, and twining his fingers through my hair. He tugs it gently, exerting an almost imperceptible pressure, tilting my head back ever so slightly. I grip the ledge and lean into his body. His kisses are warm and natural in the face of our unnatural circumstances – the differences in our age, our class, our situation. He runs his hand along my freshly razored leg, dancing it lightly over my handiwork – grazing my calf and cresting the cap of my knee. His caress is one of courteously passionate detection, forceful at the same time that it's cautiously respectful. He moves his hands higher, stroking my thigh, and I lay mine over his. Hold them there. Bring my legs together, lowering them over the edge and turning my body towards him. I slowly slide them apart – the silent answer to a question he has never bothered to ask. *Yes, it is okay.*

CHAPTER TWELVE

The welcoming V of my thighs draws him towards me. I wrap my legs around his waist and he lifts me from the ledge, supporting me with a single arm as he carries me to the opposite end of the balcony. We fall through a door and onto the bed, the weight of his body pinning me to the mattress. His hands slide down my side, and I twist to accommodate his request – allow him to slip my dress above my hips and pull my underwear the length of my legs.

And then, he pauses – hovering above me – he bends down, and my breath catches, uncertain as to what will happen next. Defying my expectations, he plants a single kiss on my stomach – the area just below my belly button – directly in the middle of my hips. Suddenly, the room stops spinning, and all of my self-conscious thoughts spill back into my half-drunken head. I feel every tendon of my body tense. He's touching *it* – his lips are touching it. That which is never to be noticed by anyone but me. I hate this spot, and I hate the idea of any man having to touch it, especially Jack.

And yet, this is the place that he touches, and this is the place that he kisses. He kisses it as he works his fingers inside me, plying my diffident frame with the long languid strokes I use on myself. With the touch of a woman, or a man who knows a woman's body. An act of worship that makes it easier to bear the indignity of surrender without feeling silly and sentimental. I relax again. Feel the springs of my subconscious begin to uncoil. My inhibitions flowing out through the fingertips of palms spread open on the sheets. They say, *I give up*. I give in.

Jack is the first man to go down on me – ever – and he eats me the way one would an oyster, like a delicacy to be savoured, not devoured. He cups his hands around me, and brings me to his lips. Drinks in the softest part of me with tender force. It feels pure. Free from the anxious desperation I've always associated with empty gratification. He doesn't give begrudgingly, a gift that hinges on the hope of one in return. Unlike those before him, Jack never places a suggestive hand on the back of my head – never uses force to force my hand. His are the ones that do the work, and bringing my legs over his shoulders, he gently eases my thighs apart. I wind a softly curved calf about his back – permitting his presence inside me – urging him on with the flex of my thigh and my fingers digging into his forearms.

He leans into me now – and each thrust doesn't push our bodies apart, but rather draws them closer together – fusing us in a single slow rolling wave of silence and sound. As his hips drive harder, the pace of his breath quickens, and I feel the tension in his body break. A liquid warmth fills the polyurethane pouch pressed against my insides, and I know then that it's over. I breathe, gasping for air, and the breath fills my entire body – oxygen rushing to my head and my heart. Jack releases a slow shuddering sigh and falls to the bed beside me. Lies still. Silent. Speechless.

Flat on my back, my chest rises and falls in rapid succession, my spine tingling with sensation. Jack runs a single hand along the corrugated plane of my sternum – passing it through the widely spaced valley of my breasts. He lingers there, and I look down. I see his hand and, in that moment, I realize I've forgotten to feel hatred for myself. For my body. For the asymmetry of my breasts. My stomach. I've forgotten to feel anything at all; and, for that, I love him.

✧

A few hours later, I awake. I feel disoriented until I remember where I am. In the morning light, everything looks different; but then, I probably never really saw the room at all. The clock beside the bed reads 6:03 a.m. I hadn't meant to spend the night – have never slept in bed with a man before. I feel uncomfortable, my body stiff with sex and exertion. My tongue stale and furry. I have a sudden urge to be gone. To return to the safe haven of my own home to sort my thoughts out, but I'm not sure how best to do this. I'm trapped. Jack lies on his stomach beside me, his face turned away and his arm resting on my lower abdomen. I press myself into the mattress and attempt to slide out from underneath him, easing myself over the edge of the bed in a single seamless motion.

"Where do you think you're going?" he asks, taking me by surprise as he grips my arm.

"To the bathroom," I reply, twisting free of his grasp. "I'll be right back."

He rolls over onto his back and props himself up on some pillows, a sheet pulled haphazardly across his nakedness.

"Stop," he says, raising his hand. "Stay there."

I stop. Smile. Obey, without knowing why.

"Turn," he says.

I pirouette in place, the shafts of early morning light playing off the pale planes of my skin. My arms dance about me like the thin ropey ribbons of a Maypole. I slow, swaying slightly. "What was that for?"

"You have absolutely no idea," he says. "Do you?"

"About what?" I ask.

"You," he says. "You're perfect."

I laugh nervously, suddenly aware of how naked I am in his eyes. "Right," I reply, "Just give me a mirror and I'll give you about a million faults. There are so many things I would wish away. There are so many things I wish you couldn't see."

"Come here," he says, patting the sheet beside him. I crawl back into bed, lying against the arm he lays across my pillow. "You know what I love about you?" he asks, toying with my nipple, plucking it gently until it grows rosebud pink and hard. "I love...*this* nipple," he smiles. "It's so you. No other woman has the same one, and yet most men probably never notice it. It's completely unique, but overlooked, just like one of your crazy photos, I guess."

"What do you mean?" I ask, a little surprised that he's even remembered. I didn't really think he'd been listening.

"Well, take a woman," he says, "any woman. If you admire her for what's there – what's obvious – it's too easy. It's sharing something she's shared with so many others. But if you take what isn't there – the hidden – then you know you're touching something truly untouched. Unique. To me, that's sexy."

I consider this a moment in silence. "I wish more men felt the way you do," I reply. "Or more women – about themselves."

"The only thing that makes something special is its being seen," he says. "That's all."

"Seen and seen as desirable," I reply, correcting him. "That's the key."

"Desire is a complicated thing, Grace. I think most women misunderstand it. We're all pretty selfish beings. Men. Women. You name it," he says. "Often, the image we're attracted to isn't the one we see, but the one we see in their eyes. There's no such thing as unselfish desire."

"You really believe that?" I ask. *Then what does that say about you? About me?*

He rolls me towards him with a squeeze of my shoulder, and plants a kiss on my forehead.

"You're perfect, Grace. Don't let anyone tell you otherwise," he says. "Not even yourself."

I just smile. His words sound so sweet, I don't bother trying to decipher the meaning behind them. Don't worry that he hasn't answered my question. I turn into his embrace and find his lips with mine. "Thank you," I reply, "for everything."

He answers with another kiss – an appreciative squeeze of my bum.

"And now," I ask, "may I go to the bathroom?"

He laughs, releasing his hold on my shoulders.

"Of course," he says, falling back against the sheet. "Knock yourself out."

CHAPTER THIRTEEN

"Grace!" my mom calls, "over here." She's easy to spot in a crowd, not only because she's so tall, but because she's so striking. She's wiry – waif-like – usually without a stitch of makeup, just the faintest fringe of black mascara around deeply set green eyes. She waves her arm – a steady self-controlled arc – as though carrying out a series of choreographed movements. "I was getting worried," she says. "I thought you were going to be late."

"No, you didn't," I reply. "You assumed I would be."

"Please, Grace," she says. "You know I can't stand semantics." She glides towards me in a swath of shimmering silver – sharply bobbed grey hair and a well-tailored grey suit. Long ropes of silver chains snake down the flat plain of her chest, resting on a white silk camisole. As usual, she is the essence of sophisticated simplicity. "I've been calling you all afternoon," she says. "I've told you before, I don't appreciate my calls going unanswered on a phone *I* pay for. Where were you?"

"Out," I reply. I hate dignifying my mother's presumptuous requests with a response. *It's none of her business where I've been, and certainly not what I've been doing...with whom.*

"Out?" she repeats. "Does that pass for an answer these days?"

"Shouldn't we get inside," I try. "I think I saw some friends of yours in the lobby." I gaze over her right shoulder to lend my claim an air of veracity.

"Very well," she says. "Tickets, please." I produce them from my purse and hand them over. She takes both, offering mine up to the attendant as though I were a child. "She's with me," she says, resting a hand on my shoulder. I shrug it off, and take a step away to create some semblance of space between our bodies. She closes the gap in a matter of seconds, following close behind me, pulling my hair into a ponytail. She holds it in hand at the nape of my neck. "Your hair is a disgrace," she says. "Don't you have an elastic with you?"

"No, I don't," I reply, wresting it from her grasp. "Besides, I like it this way."

I hadn't even had time to shower, let alone wash my hair – although I did manage a wardrobe change. Still exhausted, I'd only managed to drag myself upstairs to fall into bed fully clothed. I slept for an hour – two, three, four. I slept until I couldn't sleep anymore, awakening in the dull heat of late afternoon, the day half gone in indolence. I can still smell him on my skin, and I don't want my mother touching my memories – tainting them.

"You're hopeless," she says, with a few condemning clucks of her tongue. "Exactly like your father. You didn't get those curls from me, or the impertinence."

"Don't worry, Mom," I reply. "Rachel has reaped the benefits of your genetic makeup." *Your legacy will live on despite my many deficiencies.* She and Rachel share the same stick-straight hair the same stick-straight personalities. My father and I share the same wavy free-form locks and free-form approach to life. My mother resents both.

"That's not entirely true," she says. "Rachel looked a little like your father too, but that was back when she was a baby. Long before you were born." There are eight years between Rachel and I, my birth being an afterthought in a marriage that had long since passed its best before date – the temporary chain that manacled my parents together for eight more. I've always felt my mother hated me by proxy, not because she didn't love me, but because she didn't really love my father, and I was the means of keeping her bound to him that much longer. His failings have always felt like my fault.

"You look nice," I say, attempting to divert her attention.

"Do I?" she asks. "I feel dreadful. I spent all night writing feedback for the medical students I'm supervising this semester. They're an abysmal lot. I thought I'd escape lengthy evaluations; but, somehow, it seems to take just as much energy to criticize as it does to praise."

"I can think of better ways to spend a Friday night," I reply. She raises a single silver brow in my direction. It says, *Watch your step*. My mother doesn't date. Never has. She says she's too old to pretend she's young enough to fall in love.

Oh, it's fine," she says. "Just work. You know how it is."

I do not. In twenty years, I've only visited her office a handful of times, mostly when I was little, and I have a sneaking suspicion I was only being trotted out as proof that her maternity leave was not an extended sabbatical. "Besides, I had to put the finishing touches on a paper anyway. I'm presenting at a conference tomorrow."

"Oh, yeah," I reply, happy to take the focus off of me. "What about?"

"Nothing you'd be interested in," she says, "just a bunch of doctors – medical jargon."

"Try me," I reply.

She cuts a sidelong glance at me. "Well, if you must know," she says, "I'm working on a case study. We're trying to reduce the use of general anaesthesia at the hospital. It involves a single injection into the nerve which can numb an entire limb for hours," she says. "The patient is immobilized but not unconscious. They can still function – see, hear, breathe, think – observe the procedure. They just can't feel anything."

"And this is a good thing?" I ask. "You want people to remember something terrible like surgery?"

"You'd be surprised," she replies. "Surgery isn't so bad, and I think the more aware we are of what's happening, the better our body is able to recover."

"This coming from a woman who specializes in knocking people out?"

"It's ironic, I suppose," she says, "but I'm increasingly starting to believe that our bodies know how to make sense of pain, even when it's senseless – with or without our interventions. It's an amazing organism, Grace. It's thinking all the time. Figuring things out. You'd be surprised what it's capable of sustaining. Anyway, enough about work," she says. "It's Saturday. I don't even want to think about it. How about you? Have you gotten your grades back yet?"

"No, not yet," I reply. "But I did *just* graduate. It might take some time, you know."

"Well, how long do they expect you to wait?"

"I'm sure they'll be posted soon," I reply. Behind her, I spy the softly blue-lit bar. Try yet another distraction. "I think I'll get a drink, Mom. Would you like anything? A glass of wine?"

"Yes, please. White's fine, thank you, Grace. Here," she says, "let me give you some money." She fishes through her clutch and produces a twenty dollar bill. *Right on cue.* I'm relieved. The request had been a ruse really – one I'd perfected to induce my parents to pay for dinners, lunches, brunches and bottles of wine. I wasn't proud of it, but it became a necessity when Rachel started pulling in nearly six figures. Insisting that everyone pay for their portion of the bill. This meant me. And so, when I order two glasses of white wine, I keep the change. Slip it into my pocket. Bus fare for later.

"So," my mother says, taking a slow sip of wine, "no word on your grades, but that doesn't mean you can't give any more thought to grad school."

"I told you already, Mom, I'm still not sure I want –"

"*Nonsense*, Grace," she says, waving a dismissive wrist in my direction. "I've told you before, a Master's degree is the best thing for you right now. It's a natural extension of your education. So, which are your top choices?"

"I haven't really given it any thought," I reply. "Like I said, I don't think –"

"I was speaking to a friend who works for the Gallery," she says. "She suggested we consider some of the Masters programs in Europe. Give yourself some exposure to the art itself – add some credibility to your CV. You know, get some *hands-on* experience."

The corners of my lips curl into a private smile. One intended only for Jack.

"Is there something funny about that, Grace?" she asks. "About your future?"

"No," I reply. "Sorry, my mind was somewhere else." I sip my wine, allowing the acidic coolness to coat the inside of my limbs. I can feel the tension beginning to ease, and the hairs on the back of my neck stand down as I roll those two fateful words over my tongue. *My future.* Usually, they make me anxious and panicky, particularly when they're coming from my mother's mouth. It is never an open-ended proposition, but an either/or one – this Master's program or that one. However, today, the bite of indecision is tempered with the memory of last night's well-chosen choices, and I can let my mother talk because I cannot hear her.

"This is important, Grace," she says. "I'm not the one applying for school, you know."

"Then why do you keep saying *we?*"

She stares into my eyes, and I meet her gaze, measure for measure. "Grace, there's no need to get your back up," she says. "I'm just trying to be helpful."

"Mom, I really don't feel like talking about this right now," I reply. "I told you, when I know, you'll know. I promise. You'll be the first phone call."

"Have you spoken to your father about it?" she asks, momentarily placated. "I should be amused to hear what his opinion is on the subject."

"He's been out of town," I reply. "I haven't had a chance." It makes no difference anyway. I already know what my father will say – the same thing he's been saying my entire life. *Gracie, whatever you want is fine. I just want you to be happy.* Great. Happy. A single destination with no directions. I appreciate the sentiment, but it's about as useful as my mother's overbearing overtures. "He's fine with whatever I decide. He just wants me to be happy."

The hard lines of her face soften, a slackening so understated it's taken me almost two decades to discern it. She clasps my shoulders and spins me towards her. Grips my upper arms between the hard wires of her hands.

"I want you to be happy too, Grace," she says. "You know I do, but I can't sugar-coat things the way your father does. It's not my way."

"Mom, I –"

"Education is the best way to secure your future," she says. "Trust me. When you're on your own – independent, like Rachel – then I can rest easy. I'll know my job is done."

I take another sip of wine. Remain silent. *There's no point. She simply doesn't get it.* I've never really understood my mother, and I doubt very much that she has understood me. We're closer than my father and I, but only in proximity; our relationship held together with the glue of status quo and statutory holidays. It isn't necessarily a superficial bond, but it does live at the surface – always skating over what should be a genuine emotional exchange.

"It's time," she says, as the lights dim, telling us to take our seats. I tilt my head back and drain my wine in a single gulp, depositing the empty glass in a nearby planter. Behind me, my mother pushes me towards the entrance, clicking her tongue in disapproval.

✧

We take our seats, sandwiched between two elderly couples, fossils from a land before time. Seated at my mother's elbow, I feel about twelve years old, and am eager for this entire experience to be over. "So, who's performing?" I ask.

"A young cellist," my mother says, "a solo artist. I've never heard him before. He's from Russia. Supposed to be quite good."

"Really?" I ask, my interest in the evening suddenly piqued. I've never seen a solo cellist before, although I've always longed to. I feel a secret affinity for the oversized string instrument – so often overlooked – made to stand down in deference to the daintier violins, relegated to the back of the orchestra pit. Now, it stands alone, propped up by unseen hands in a solitary circle of light. I consider its warm wood face, and admire the deep etching on the heavily scrolled head, the long tapered neck, the hairpin curves of its maple-hued body. The strings are tightly wound against the fingerboard – waiting in silent expectation for the firm caress of fingers that will bring them to life.

I think of Jack, and a warm flush of remembrance emanates from the depths of my sex. The thought of hands that hold the power to awaken. To enliven. To embolden. Hands that are different from any I've ever felt before. In his hands, my body sings – not because I'm particularly musical, but because he knows how to play me.

The resounding applause of the house startles me back to my senses as the performer takes the stage. He bows and flips back a pair of long black coattails, settling himself onto a simple stool. The lights dim and the stage is softly spot lit in a shaft of yellow-white light. He raises an arm, taut but not tense, the bow a natural extension of his body. *All things should be so easy*, I think. *All passions so organically conceived, culminating in the pursuit of a profession you were born for, not bred for.*

In the dark, my mother sits beside me – her arm so close I can feel its heat and the hairs against my own. *She doesn't see things this way,* I think. *She doesn't understand.*

The cellist touches down, string to string, and saws through the first few strains of Bach's Suite No. 1. From that simple instrument, he coaxes the most complex subtleties of intonation imaginable. His face serene, his eyes closed, he leans into the instrument, and I can see the precise moment when his body no longer ends where it used to, but starts where it should. *He gets it,* I think. *He understands.*

Afterwards, my mother and I stand together outside the theatre. There's a slight chill in the evening air, and I wrap my arms across my chest, hugging myself to keep from growing cold.

"No sweater?" she asks.

"Guess not," I reply. "I forgot."

"I should have known," she said. "Ever since you were a little girl, forgetting things." She runs her hand over my hair and I sidestep her caress. She demurs, dropping it back to her side. "I forgot to mention, I heard from Rachel," she says. "Did she call you too?"

"I must have missed her," I reply. "What did she say?"

"They offered her the position," she says. "I expected as much. She starts in September."

"Really?" I ask, my intestines wrapping themselves around my spine. "You must be happy."

"Me?" she repeats. "Whatever does it have to do with me? I'm happy for Rachel – if it's what she wants."

"Of course," I reply, a little too quickly. "It's great." The rabbit's warren of soft wrinkles around her eyes loosens, and she rubs my arm. This time, I don't bother batting her away. I imagine the gesture is supposed to generate some feeling of warmth, but all I feel is cold – goose pimples rapidly proliferating along the back of my arm.

"Don't worry, Grace," she says. "You'll get there."

I purse my lips and nod. I nod even though I cannot recall saying I was worried. *Typical.* My mother. Rachel. They both think they know what to expect. What I'm thinking. What I'm feeling. What I'll do. Who I'll be. *I'm so sick of it.* Sick of the sense that I'm always living up to their expectations rather than just living.

"What are you talking about?" I ask. "Who said I was worried?"

"You're great too, Grace," she says. "You just have different gifts than Rachel. Different strengths. You have to find a way to put them to use, that's all."

I feign a smile. Say nothing. This type of unsolicited demi-compliment is characteristic of my mother. She's a doctor – a scientist. Everything and everyone stands in comparison to someone else and there are only a finite number of commendations to be doled out. Accolades come in fractions – highly coveted slices of a single pie that can only be cut so many times. Each compliment given to Rachel means one less for me. The sad kind of heart math that inevitably leaves someone to go hungry.

"Can I give you a ride home?" she asks. "I'm going right by the house."

"No, I'll be fine," I reply. "I have bus fare." I slip my hands into the pockets of my dress, wrapping my fingers around the coins. Rub the lightly brailed faces. "I don't need a ride."

"Honestly, Grace, I don't like the thought of you taking the bus alone at this time of night," she says. "It's not safe."

"I said, I'm fine," I repeat. "I'll find my own way."

"All right," she says. "Suit yourself. But I could drop you off right at your doorstep."

Thanks, Mom, but really – I don't need a ride." After all, *I have no intention of going home.*

CHAPTER FOURTEEN

Stepping off the bus, I follow the lights like a moth to the flame, compelling my feet to move despite the misgivings in my mind. The gate is already drawn back, and the windows burn softly in the dark – dull orange hearts beating through the blackened embers of the evening sky. The door swings wide after the second knock, as though he'd known I'd come – as though he'd been waiting all along.

"Grace," Jack says, with a slight nod – a smile. He steps aside to let me in, strains of jazz slipping past and dancing out onto the front steps. "Come on in."

"I'm sorry for just showing up like this," I say. "I would've called but I don't have my cell phone." As proof, I pat the empty pockets of my dress. "I was just out for a walk. Is it a bad time?"

"Not at all," he says. "I was just packing for my trip. My flight's first thing tomorrow."

"Oh, right. Of course. I remember." I hadn't, but I do now. He's leaving for Europe. Business of an indeterminate nature. For an indeterminate length of time. I swallow hard, my throat lightly salted with the first stirrings of bile. I feel nauseous. Nervous. But I don't know why. Shuffle from one sandalled foot to the other.

"I'm glad you stopped by," Jack says. "I was just thinking about you."

"Really?" I ask. Again, I shift from one foot to the other, running my hand the length of my opposite arm. It itches, like bugs crawling underneath my skin. I want to look at him but I can't bring myself to meet his gaze.

"Are you okay?" he says. "You look a little…something. Do you want to talk about it?"

I look up then, realizing for the first time just how close his face is to mine. *Physical intimacy is a funny thing.* To release yourself so completely into the hands of another human being without knowing how much they're capable of holding. *To hold is one thing. To support is another.* I cannot really say why it doesn't seem right to tell him about Rachel. About my mother. About any of it. It just doesn't fit in the box I've built for myself. It just isn't right.

"I'm fine," I reply. "Just tired."

"Well, here," he says, reaching for the strap of my purse, "let me take your bag."

I catch his hand mid-air and grasp it tightly. I meet his gaze – his eyes a question mark as I guide his hand to my chest – forcing a rough squeeze of my breast. I reach for his face. Bite his lower lip, silencing his words with the weight of my kisses. Everything seems to hinge on his not speaking. *I don't want him to talk. I don't want to talk.* I want to blow everything wide open. To blow it all apart.

He doesn't take much provocation, and picking up the tenor of my touch, he finds the tune. I bring my arms over my head and he strips me in the foyer – my layers peeled back like the skin of a banana – white flesh laid bare, marred only by a few bruises from the night before. His hands slide down my back – pitch perfect as they snake up my spine and wrap themselves around my rib cage. I wind my legs about his waist, and the loops of his belt bite into the soft underside of my thighs. He lifts me from the ground and my back brushes against the wall. Now, the blunt edge of a doorway. Finally, the cool kiss of kitchen counter granite on my bare legs.

I try to help with his belt buckle. I want to. *I want it*, but everything happens too fast, and there aren't enough seconds in a minute. Not enough space between our bodies, the distance shrinking even further as he draws me sharply towards him. He sets me on my feet, but I land mostly on his, and I fumble to find a foothold on the floor. Hands on hips spin me round in a swift jerking motion and a skilled arm levers me over the counter, my breasts flattening with a slightly sickening *smack*.

I can hear his teeth tearing at the package of a foil wrapped condom, and I briefly consider the implications of sleeping with someone who carries condoms in his pockets. *Is this what they mean by safe sex?* I wonder. *Perhaps.*

I brace myself as he enters me, the stiff upper lip of the countertop eating into my hips. Standing on tip-toe, I raise myself up so that the long angular *L* of my body forms a perpendicular plane against his. Precise. Perfunctory. My hands search for something they can grasp – instinct taking hold where best intentions left off – but I come up empty-handed. I am without moorings, and yet I'm pinned in place – out of my depth, and into his. The dull pounding thud of him presses against the inside of my bones, and something inside me wants to say, *Stop*, but only if I can find a way to make it mean, *Keep going*. I want the pressure to abate; but, at the same time, I fear what will fill the void. And so, I just push back.

Jack shudders then – slouches forward, pressing me between himself and the counter like a late autumn leaf between two bricks. He releases a long slow breath, and runs his hand the length of my arm, tingling to life as pins and needles ricochet through my bloodless limbs. I feel spent, despite the fact that I've exerted no effort – teary-eyed and exhausted. *Perhaps this is how it's supposed to feel,* I think. *Perhaps this is it – all the way.*

✧

In the bathroom, I flip the switch, light illuminating the tiny powder room. I hear Jack pad down the hall towards the bedroom, and I close the door. Lock it. Turn the water on and let it run to cover a slight cough as I regain my composure. Glancing up, I look into the mirror. My eyes are darkly raccooned with mascara and my face is flushed. I look so strange. Not like myself. Not like *that girl*. And yet, *There she is*. I can tell by the eyes, but even those seem slightly different tonight. Ordinarily, the granite-hued striations pinwheel about my pupils like a foxtrot twirl of tulle. Now, they have the lazy sway of sea grass, the dull centres slack and lifeless like little ships lost at sea.

I splash some water on my cheeks, and pat them dry with a charcoal-coloured hand towel. Leave a few streaks of makeup in my wake, and guiltily fold it back the other way, replacing it on the rack. I run my fingers through my hair but can't seem to untangle the snarled mess my mother had tried to tame earlier that evening. Silently curse myself for never being prepared – never having a hair tie when I need it most.

I crack the door on Jack's medicine cabinet and I'm not surprised to find what I'm looking for, although I'd secretly hoped I might not: a stash of hair elastics in a neat little pile on the top shelf. Something so simple and seemingly insignificant that says so much. *You are not the only one. You are not special.*

I choose a red one at random, the cast off item of some other woman from some other time. *Who was she?* I wonder. Who *is* she? Someone serious or someone just for fun? *Someone like me.* I take the tie in my hands, stretch it out and wrap it around my wrist. Snap it once or twice. Study the red mark that wells up beneath it. *Maybe it's the illusion that makes it so intriguing. If it's fake – if I'm one of a few or one of a million – does that make it feel less good? Does it diminish the intoxicating effects of desire? If something is so disposable, does that mean it's not worth having in the first place?* I smooth my hands over my hair and pull it into a ponytail, close the cabinet, and switch the light off. Make my way down the hall where I know that Jack is waiting.

In the bedroom, he's already turned the sheets back and switched on a soft yellow lamp. Again, the room looks entirely different, and I wonder at its ability to transform itself from one moment to the next. Jack beckons me forward and I crawl in beside him. He pulls me towards him, my back pressed tight against his chest.

"I've got to leave tomorrow," he whispers into my shoulder. "You know that, right?" The moon sends slivers of light through the bedroom windows, and they land on my limp frame, my body stretched to match the length of his. I face the mirror located directly across from the bed. I take the photo with my mind. Two bodies. Lifeless, languid and inert. *Ecstasy*? I want to say it, but I know it isn't right. And yet, I have no other words. No other emotions. Only emptiness – a sensation of supreme loneliness and fatigue.

"But I'll be thinking about you," he breathes. His hand slides down my arm – mounts my hip, and comes to a rest on my sex, gently cradling its soft heat. It's the careful caress of a child, cupping a baby bird that has fallen from its nest. "I'll be thinking about this."

What is it about a stranger stroking the softest part of us that seems so insincere? Does love always have to have a familiar face? I breathe deeply, the air escaping my lungs for what feels like the first time since I set foot in his house. I want to speak – to second his emotion – but I can't. No words come to match his. I don't have the map to navigate these waters – the nether regions of naked desire – and now, all I feel is stupid for ever thinking I was strong enough to swim in the deep end. Woman enough. I feel the tears trying to come, but shame myself into staving them off. In all of my twenty-two years, I've never felt so foolish. Never felt so young.

Where are the people who really know me? I stare into the mirror without seeing, and I think of Rachel then. Wonder where she is and what she's doing. Celebrating, no doubt. I realize I wish she'd wanted to share the moment with me too. To tell me the news herself. But she hadn't.

Jack kisses my shoulder again, bringing me back to both the moment and myself. "Stay the night?" he asks. "I'd like you to."

It's a question I know I will not answer out loud. Instead, I simply turn into his embrace, curling myself into his stomach in silent assent. *Yes, I'll stay.* After all, I have absolutely nowhere else to be.

CHAPTER FIFTEEN

"Geez, what gives?" Eli cries, as I shatter my second saucer of the day.

Shit. "I know," I reply. "I'm sorry. Let me pay you back for them. Take it out of my cheque or something."

"No, don't worry. It's not that," he says. "It's just, you seem distracted. You okay?"

"Of course," I say. "Everything's fine." This is the truth, so far as I know it. Or, so far as I want to. True, I have been feeling a little dizzy this morning…well, this week, but it's nothing. Probably just a few too many missed breakfasts. And then, there are the cramps – the abdominal pain – but I'm probably just getting my period. Or a bladder infection. Maybe a yeast infection. Whatever it is, it's no big deal. *Just girl stuff.* Ordinarily, I would talk to Ilena about it. Maybe even Rachel in a pinch. But they are both gone. Have both abandoned me.

"If you say so," Eli replies, "but you look a little green around the gills. Have you checked a mirror lately?" He disappears into the back, and I crouch down to collect the shards of porcelain, placing them in my open palm. I clip my finger on one, and a single spot of blood pools up – filling the fleshy whorls of my fingertip.

"Fuck," I say, under my breath. Eli returns from the back with a dustpan and broom. "Here, let me," I say, reaching for it with one hand and bringing the other to my mouth.

"No, I'll do it," he replies. "Hey, are you bleeding?"

"It's nothing," I reply, "just a tiny cut."

"Well, you'll have to get a Band-Aid," he says. "Check the back." For once, I obey without argument, and make my way towards the staff bathroom, which also doubles as the First Aid station. I tug the chain-link cord that hangs from the naked bulb, and the windowless closet is bathed in a vile yellow light. Above the sink, the medicine cabinet houses our "First-Aid supplies" – a single box of Band-Aids and a bottle of antiseptic. Eli's always been the type of guy who thinks there's nothing a hastily fashioned T-shirt tourniquet can't take care of.

Eli. As I reach for the mirror door, his words return to haunt me. *Have you checked a mirror lately?* I haven't, but I do now. Cannot avoid it. I stare into its depths – into mine, and the image mocks me. Eli is right. *I do look like hell.* I place my hands on the side of the washstand, gripping the edges in a white-knuckled embrace. *Now or never,* I say to myself.

I have to admit that I can feel it – the cool smooth surface of the sink pulsating under the pressure of my palms. *I have to admit that I can feel it* – the thin line of perspiration that snakes down my spine, winding its way between the hairs that dust my dorsal ridge. *I have to admit that I can feel it* – the same feeling all week – a slight tingling sensation. A flicker of pain that lingers but a moment before dying out.

Tingling. That's precisely what it feels like. Ordinarily, I associate this word with good things. *Sparkles. Snowflakes. Sleigh bells. Sex.* But this isn't like any of those. This is a persistent burning sensation, increasing in intensity as time goes by. At first, I ignored it. Silenced the voice of intuition that accompanied it. A new voice – a voice even older than my own. It sings out from somewhere behind my belly button. A single refrain uttered over and over for none to hear but me. All week long, it has woken me up from nightmares and snapped me out of daydreams. It calls me. It sings, and it says, *Something is not right.*

"Maybe you're right," I say, wrapping the Band-Aid around the end of my finger. Eli is still on the floor, sweeping up the remains of my latest fumble.

"What?"

"Maybe you're right," I repeat, "about me. I'm not feeling so hot today...for the past few days actually. I should probably just pop over to the clinic or something," I say, shrugging my shoulders. "Do you think I could leave early?"

"Of course," he replies. "Is there anything I can do? I mean, are you okay?"

"I'll be fine," I say. "It's nothing. Probably *girl stuff.*"

"Right," Eli replies. "Enough said. Go. Take the day."

"Thanks, Eli." Most men won't challenge menstrual matters. Eli is an oddity to be sure; but, in this, he is no exception. "I'll be back bright and early tomorrow."

"No, you won't," he says. "It's Saturday. You're not scheduled."

"Shit, you're right," I say. "I totally forgot."

Saturday. Nearly one week since Jack left. I hadn't even realized. Nearly one week since he'd dropped me off outside my house. We'd had no tearful parting. No passionate embrace. Nothing to match the amorous heights we'd already reached. I didn't move to kiss him, and he didn't move to stop me. He just smiled. Let me know not to expect him any time soon. *Shouldn't be more than two or three weeks*, he'd said. *Maybe a month. You know how these deals can go sideways sometimes.* I didn't, but I was starting to get a vague idea.

"Name and date of birth at the top," the attendant drawls. She pushes a clipboard across the counter towards me. I clasp it between two clammy hands, my eyes skimming the sheet. *West Broadway Walk-In Medical Clinic.* The block letters float above a sea of subtly vibrating black lines. They blur and intersect as I try to focus.

"Don't forget your health card number," she says. "The rest should be pretty self-explanatory."

"Thanks," I reply, eager to sit. Not to be standing as the centre of attention at the desk. I lower myself onto a standard-issue plastic waiting room chair – uncomfortably sterile, uncomfortably uncomfortable. I glance down. The lines and spaces still swim together. I look back up. Scan the faces of my companions.

There's an elderly woman with a pink protrusion on her eyelid. A snot-nosed child with its mother, nursing its thumb. I feel out of place, mostly because I don't look sick. Just a little pale. These people should be here, but not me. Outside, the young summer sky is grey with indecision, uncertain as to whether it should rain or not – filled with the promise of pouring if it does.

I turn my attention back to the form. *When was your last full physical check-up?* Good question. I've never been a person who sees physicians with any regularity, besides my mother of course; and she had always eschewed formal medical examinations in favour of impromptu and very public check-ups at social functions – calling me to her side to loudly question a slight cough. I get the distinct impression that these displays are meant to be demonstrations of her medical skill and so-called maternal affection, more than serious attempts to suss out some malady. As such, I've never placed much store in the profession. Clinics are my preferred mode of medical diagnosis, and I only hope that this one will live up to its Walk-in and subsequent Walk-*out* policy. I want to get this over with quickly. Painlessly.

"You missed one," the receptionist says. She rests a red nail polished finger on a blank line, obscuring the field of text. "Reason for visit," she says. "You've got to list one."

"It's personal," I reply.

She eyes me. Her pen poised above the line. Waiting. "Honey, this is a walk-in clinic," she says. "Everything's personal. You'll have to be a little more specific."

"I think I have a bladder infection," I lie, lowering my voice. "Or something."

"We'll need a urine sample then," she says. Reaching beneath the counter, she produces a plastic cup. "Take this to the bathroom. End of the hall."

"Thanks," I reply, my cheeks burning with indignation. Tests are for sick people, and I'm not sick. I pocket the cup, avoiding the curious gazes. Shielding myself from the puss-laced pity of the elderly woman. I will not be lumped among them – the walking wounded – I will not be worthy of their sympathy. I don't need it. Don't need anything from anyone.

CHAPTER SIXTEEN

I emerge from the bathroom, and make my way back down the hall, depositing the vial at the desk. Palming it off like a piece of contraband. The receptionist eyes me suspiciously, as though I've been lining my pockets with pink liquid soap and free toilet paper.

"Second door on your right," she says, glancing over the top of her glasses. "There's a paper gown on the table. The doctor will be right with you."

I'm naked, nothing but a gaping gown separating me from the paper-covered table. I swing my legs over the edge, my feet almost touching the floor. I clasp my hands together, and bring them to rest in the paper nest between my thighs. Glance around at four formerly white walls. Stainless steel countertops. The halogen lights hum overhead, and a wall-mounted clock counts off the seconds. Marking time. Counting down. *To what?* That, I don't yet know.

Nearly thirty minutes pass before I hear the metallic rattle of my chart being withdrawn from its holster. A cold gust of air ushers in a mid-sized middle-aged Asian man. Black hair. White coat. A burgundy tie with yellow checks. Fresh-faced.

Professional. Not yet embittered by the walk-in clinic beat. Not like some others I've seen, or who have seen me.

He introduces himself as Dr. Yu, and alights on a rolling stool, knees bowed outward, feet bowed in. One hand rests on the ledge between his legs, giving him the appearance of a frog in a lab coat atop a lily pad. He moors himself near my exposed knee cap. Consults my chart. I clear my throat, and pull at the *papier maché* hem of my gown.

"So, what can we do for you today...Grace?" he asks. "It says here you have a bladder infection, but I've just seen your urinalysis results and they appear normal. Have you been having any other symptoms?" he asks, more of his tie than of me. "Pain. Fever. Vaginal discharge. Burning during urination?"

I want to answer, but all I can think of is how naked I feel – not the good kind. Not like with Jack. Just me. Naked. Exposed. I feel hollow – like the shell of myself is sitting here, rather than me. Perspiration beads on my brow and my nostrils flare slightly, my breathing growing shallow. I shake my head, *No. None of those symptoms.* Dr. Yu glances up. I feel myself grow tense, but as my countenance grows firmer, his begins to soften.

"Okay, Grace, now let's just have a look here," he says. He jettisons himself to the far end of the examination table. Produces a hidden set of stirrups. "Why don't we get you to lie down," he says, patting the padded edge. I obediently comply – his *we*-ing making my resistance seem futile. We have already decided. I lift my legs, plant my palms on either side of my hips and pivot in place. Lie back – my paper gown whispering drily against the table cloth.

"Now, Grace, just set your heels here," he says, guiding my feet towards the metal stirrups. I allow him to do so, but tent my hands over my abdomen, jealously guarding my stomach. Lock myself in a staring contest with the ceiling tiles. Fixate on the delicate filigree of finite holes that dot its surface. Clench my jaw. Listen to the sound of my teeth grinding in my ears.

"I'm just going to do a routine pelvic exam, Grace," Dr. Yu says, "nothing to worry about." He punctuates this with a rubber glove *snap* that sounds exactly like trouble. Nothing good ever comes from gloves. They're used to ward off contagion – contamination of a healthy body by an unhealthy one. To protect him from me.

"Now, we just need you to relax, Grace. Let your knees fall open. Imagine a beach ball between your thighs," he says. "That helps some people."

Beach ball. Beaches. Beach thoughts. I try to relax. I do. Try to think relaxing beach thoughts. But I can't stop thinking about Dr. Yu. I can't stop thinking about what he thinks. Can't stop seeing what he sees…the upturned V of two pink thighs, peaked against a stark white sheet. Headless. Bodiless. An anonymous specimen to be examined and diagnosed.

"That's great, Grace," he says. "You're doing great." He lowers himself between my thighs, the top of his dark head disappearing beneath the paper swag that hangs from knee to knee. Sets my heart beating like a hammer in my chest.

"Now, just stay put," he says, spinning towards the far wall, his back to me. He extracts a plastic-wrapped packet from a drawer. Breaks the seal. Withdraws what looks like an oversized Q-Tip. "I want to run a few more tests," he says, "so I need a swab of your vagina."

I want to ask questions. I want to speak, but the words stick in a sodden lump at the back of my throat. I turn the screws of my jaw a little tighter. Twist my face towards the wall. Wince slightly at the sharp pinching sensation. It feels like Dr. Yu is snipping a swatch of fabric from my flesh.

"I'm sorry," he says. "It might hurt a little." He withdraws the apparatus and snaps the lid on. Lays it on the counter and retrieves my chart. "You can go ahead and sit up now, Grace."

I do so – slowly, stiffly – joint by joint. Limb by limb. I draw my legs to my chest and deposit them back over the edge. Place my hands on either side. Say nothing.

"Do you have a family doctor?" he asks. "You haven't listed one here."

I shake my head. *No*, no family doctor – just a doctor in the family.

"How many sexual partners do you currently have?" he asks, his pen poised. Hovering hesitantly. "I know it seems personal, but it's important. Do you have a boyfriend?"

No, I shake my head. "I was seeing someone though – briefly."

"Practicing safe sex I assume," he says, "condoms or some other kind of protection?"

"Yes," I reply. "Of course." *Protection.* The irony of this word makes a sort of morbid laughter bubble up deep within me. Sitting here in this paper gown, I've never felt less protected – more vulnerable – less safe.

"This next question may be a little tough, Grace, but I have to ask," he says. "Did you not notice the lesions in your vaginal area? They're quite…obvious."

"I don't know," I reply. "Maybe." A hot flush of shame colours my cheeks. *Maybe I had noticed them – felt them. So what?*

"Well, Grace, we won't know for certain until we have your results," he says, "but I'm quite certain you have genital herpes."

Genital Herpes.

The two words hang in the air between us. I stare at them. Fixate on their lines and edges. The fatly rounded *G*, clashing with the right-angled *H*. My eyes glaze over. My body too. Ensconced. Cocooned in a thick syrupy silence. A sense-dulling dose of denial.

"Grace?" Dr. Yu asks. "Are you listening? We have to discuss what this means."

The doctor is talking. I know he is, but only because his lips won't lie still. His mouth is forming sounds and those sounds are forming words, but none of them make sense. Words I've always known but never put together. Words I can define but not in relation to myself. Skin. Blisters. Lesions. Scabs. Outbreak. Symptoms. Severe. Sex. Virus. Virulent. Incurable.

Incurable.

This is the one that gets me – the last one – the final knock-out punch. I move to stand, but find my legs don't work. An icy river of blood migrates from my face to my toes, and I taste the taste that grey makes on your tongue. The cold linoleum kiss of Dr. Yu's tiled floor. And then, the screen fades to black. The steady metronomic beating of my heart fills my head – a seemingly impartial referee, counting out the seconds before I am officially declared dead. One. Two. Three. Four. Five. Six. Seven. Eight. Nine. Te–

CHAPTER SEVENTEEN

"I'm glad you called," she says. "Although you should have come to me."

"I didn't call," I correct her. "The doctor did." It's early evening, and a silvery summer rain falls from a lightly bruised sky. The windshield wipers slide across the front of my mother's Lexus. I look on. Stare blankly out the window. Think about nothing in particular…everything in general.

"Well, I'm still glad," she says. "But what do you mean by going to that ridiculous clinic, Grace? For Christ's sake, I'm a doctor."

I remain silent. I could respond, but I don't want to. I don't want to tell her that Dr. Yu only called her because she was my *In Case of Emergency* person. The prerequisite filler for an otherwise empty blank. I don't tell her that I'd only done so because there was no one else. Because Ilena was in New York. Because I didn't know where my father was. Because Rachel had abandoned me. Because Jack was in France.

"Grace? Are you listening to me?" she asks. "I don't want you going to places like that. If you have a problem, whatever it is, you come to me."

Silence.

"Fine," she continues, "whatever you want, but I know it all so you might as well tell me the rest – your side. You don't have to, but you can if you want…if you don't want."

"Really?" I ask, taken aback by her uncharacteristic display of diplomacy.

"Of course," she replies. "I'm here for you – whatever you need."

"Fine then," I say, "the last one. The not talking one."

She purses her lips. Exhales audibly. I catch a glimpse of her face in the rear view mirror and feel torn. I want to continue punishing her, but she'd come to get me, so I throw her a conversational bone.

"There's nothing to tell," I say. "I just felt a little light-headed is all."

Silence.

Silence.

Swish.

Silence.

"I feel fine," I repeat. "He was being cautious. Thought it'd be better if I had a ride."

"Have you eaten today?"

"No," I reply, realizing this is true. "I forgot."

"Well, we're stopping then."

"No, thanks," I reply. "I have food at home."

"Grace, please don't argue with me," she says. "In the first place, I'm quite certain that's not true; and, in the second, you have to eat. It's not up for discussion."

I move my lips in protest, but no words come out. I fall back against my seat. Return to staring out the window. Numb. Senseless. I can hardly connect my surroundings with the events of half an hour ago. It feels odd to be sitting here, an ordinary passenger in an ordinary car on an ordinary day. It seems to me that events that change your life should change your life. I feel cheated. *My life will never be the same; and yet, everything about it is exactly the same.* And so, I give in, if only to be different.

She continues west on Broadway. Hangs a left on Larch. Pulls into a parking spot. Idles for a few seconds before switching off the engine. The wipers stop mid-wipe, frozen at awkward angles on the windshield. I turn my head. *Of course*, I think. *I should have known.*

✧

"Hello! Welcome to White Spot," chirps the hostess. She's smiling so hard it hurts my cheeks – a button-nosed brunette in a blue blouse with a bronze name tag over her left breast. *Tiffany*. "How many are we today?"

My mom raises a well-manicured hand in the international sign for peace, and I assume she's attempting to negotiate with this envoy from the alien race of Happy People. I'm incorrect.

"Two it is," Tiffany sings. "Right this way."

My mother places a hand on my back, ushering me down an aisle of fake foliage and hunter green vinyl-covered banquettes. The restaurant is dimly lit, nearly empty at this hour on a Friday afternoon. We're trapped – caught in the dining hour doldrums.

"Here we are," Tiffany says, gesturing towards a booth, arm outstretched like Vanna White on *Wheel of Fortune*. I slide onto the bench, my mother across from me, and Tiffany hands us our menus. "We're in between shifts right now so I'll also be your server this evening," she says. "What can I get you to drink?"

"I'll take a Pepsi," my mom says. I'm surprised. My mom doesn't drink soda. She drinks mineral water from green-tinted glass bottles, sweaty with perspiration and purity. Always has. But then, it has been a while since we've eaten together.

"Coming right up," Tiffany says. "And for you?" She beams down at me. Waiting. Watching. I'm on deck, but I'm not thirsty. Not hungry. Nothing at the same time that I'm everything. It all feels frozen and surreal, and yet too bright and realistic, even in the fuzzy darkness of the restaurant. Every action feels like a feeling, even breathing. Swallowing. Not to mention making a choice. Too many options but no ways out.

Like drowning on dry land. I want to wad myself with something that will dull the pain – something that will slake the sensations.

"Strawberry shake," I say, "with extra whipped cream." Now, it is my mother's turn. I can see the surprise spread across her face like a hastily scribbled note on a sheet of paper. She raises a silver brow.

"Great choice," Tiffany coos. "My favourite."

Of course it is, I think. This girl's whole life is probably one big pink strawberry shake – everything that mine is not – at least, not anymore. I bet she cuddles with her UBC football playing boyfriend after big Friday night games – big Friday night shifts. Two straws. One strawberry shake. Untouched by diseases and dis-ease. She doesn't know what herpes is. Has no clue. At least, in this, we have something in common – Tiffany and I – both completely clueless.

"Do you know what you'd like to eat?" she asks, her pencil expectant over her pad. Most White Spot patrons already know what they want. I used to be one of these – the initiated. As a little girl, I loved the consistency of this restaurant – this ritual. I always knew what to expect, and always got what I expected. A Pirate Pack. Grilled Cheese. French Fries. Styrofoam cup of coleslaw. Neapolitan ice cream. A single chocolate coin wrapped in gold foil. All squeezed neatly aboard a cardboard pirate ship.

White Spot was a tradition, but it was also a treat. Ordinarily, my health-conscious mother would not let Rachel and me within ten paces of processed food; but, on rare occasions, we'd show up. After an early evening concert. After a late afternoon wedding. A family funeral. A neatly pressed and well-presented family of four – the perfect size and shape to fit into the cubby-sized cubicle. But after the divorce, there were no more special occasions. It was just the three of us – an odd number. We didn't fill the four-person place setting anymore – a single napkin-wrapped set of cutlery unopened – swept away by a server who could understand, unlike me, that we would only be three.

I haven't been to White Spot for many years now. Forever it seems. I can't remember when we stopped coming. Can't remember why. Most likely, Rachel and I grew too old for Pirate Packs. Most likely, grilled cheese began to taste exactly like grief, its rubbery consistency congealing on my insides like all the questions I wanted to ask but couldn't. Most likely, it stopped being a pleasurable treat and started being a painful reminder, like so many things in life.

"Maybe I should give you a moment," Tiffany says. She's looking at me for direction, so I consider her question. *What do I want?* I cannot even begin to think of an answer. A cheeseburger? A steak? A salad? A new body. A new life.

"I'm not hungry," I reply, "just the shake." Across the table, my mother gives me the look – the one that says I better order something. "Fine," I say, "I'll take a grilled cheese."

"But..." Tiffany's pretty dark brows knit together in confusion, "we only offer the grilled cheese as part of the Pirate Pack."

"I know."

"...and the Pirate pack is for children..."

Silence.

"Grace," my mother says. The look again. This time, I ignore it. I don't care. She's the one that brought me here. It's not my fault that Tiffany's world is thrown into topsy-turvy disorder, it's hers.

"That's all I want," I reply. "I don't want anything else."

"Well, maybe I can put a special order in with the kitchen," Tiffany says, playing peacemaker. "It's pretty slow so I'm sure they won't mind. And for you?"

"I'll take a Triple O Burger, please," my mom says, "with everything." Yet again, I'm all astonishment. My mother eats lightly steamed greens and grilled seafood. Salads with vinaigrette on the side. *Who is this Pepsi drinking, hamburger eating person and what has she done with my mother?* "And I'll take the fries, but I'll also have a green salad as well. Dressing on the side."

There she is.

"So," Tiffany says, "that's one grilled cheese, one Triple O Burger with the works, one side salad, one Pepsi and one strawberry shake." She runs down the list, punctuates her statement with an authoritative rap of her pencil and tears the perforated sheet from the pad.

Grilled cheese and a strawberry shake. This is my second prescription of the day; and after what Dr. Yu told me about the first, I like my odds of success with the second better.

"There are no guarantees," Dr. Yu says, scribbling down a name, date and dosage. A final ballpoint flourish as he signs on the dotted line. "This initial outbreak will probably be the worst…the most painful. Your blisters will take anywhere from two to four weeks to fully heal."

"So long?" I ask, considering the fact that it had probably taken mere minutes to contract.

"Before healing can happen, the sores have to scab over," he continues. "They can't heal while they're still open. This is the most highly contagious period of the virus, Grace. You should avoid all sexual contact."

No sexual contact. I think I nod, but can't be sure. Everything sounds like static. White noise. Now fully clothed, I sit in the metal framed chair beside the examination table. I'm in the ejection seat. The place they put you before they pack you off into the world. My head throbs slightly from my brief fainting spell. My blood pressure rises at the thought of my mother in the waiting room. I'm about to be jettisoned – shot into space on a solo mission – in my shiny new incurable sexually transmitted disease. He runs through my in-flight inventory before takeoff.

"Fever. Swollen glands. Headaches. Fatigue. Itching. Vaginal discharge. Pelvic pain," he recites. "You may experience all of these. Don't panic, Grace. These are normal symptoms."

Normal symptoms? What a fucking joke. Isn't a symptom a sign that something's wrong? Isn't it our body's way of telling us that it is time to panic? The built-in *Red Alert* button on our internal dashboard. *Break in Case of Emergency.*

"Here," he says, ripping the paper from the pad and thrusting it at me. My marching orders. "You can get this filled at your pharmacist, but remember," he says, "this is just a suppressant. As I said earlier, there's no cure. You'll carry the virus for the rest of your life, Grace. You need to educate yourself on its transmission so you can protect future partners. It's very catching."

Protect future partners? I want to laugh. *Who had protected me?* Not the condom. Not my partner. Not Jack. No one. And yet, what had I expected? I shake my head. Nod. Breathe. Something about the weight and tone of Dr. Yu's voice lets me know that it isn't the same as passing on a cold. It isn't the same as coughing on your hand before shaking someone else's. It is more serious and he says it with even more gravity.

"Your case is very common, Grace. One in four people these days; and it's a fairly common misconception that condoms protect against herpes," he says. "They don't. Any skin-to-skin contact can create a bridge for the virus, but we've been over that. I think I've covered most of the main points, but you should do some reading on your own. There's just one last thing I should point out – are you planning on having children?" he asks. "Becoming a mother?"

"What?"

"Children?" he repeats. "Do you want children?"

"I'm twenty-two," I reply, as though this should be answer enough.

"Right, well – I'll take that as a no…for now," he says, "but you should know that it can be transmitted to babies through the birth canal. Neo-natal herpes is very serious, Grace. It can be deadly. You'll probably have to have a C-section."

"I…I don't even know why you're asking me this," I reply. "I don't even know if I want children, let alone how I want to give birth to them. Do we have to talk about this right now?"

"No, not right now," he replies. "I'm just letting you know that your options are limited. It's something to consider," he says, "for your future."

My future. Suddenly, I see all the babies I'd never even thought of birthing – branded – a scarlet "H" on their foreheads. Chances I'd never known I wanted to take slip through my fingers. Doors closed. Opportunities lost. *Options limited.*

"Do you have any questions before we wrap up here, Grace?"

Yes, I do. I want to know everything. I want all the answers you haven't given me. All that's written between the lines of your useless science speak. Tell me the truth. Tell me you pity me. Tell me I'm diseased. Tell me I'm broken. Tell me why…why me?

"Grace?" Dr Yu repeats. "Do you have any questions – about the virus? I need you to at least acknowledge that you understand what I've told you."

I can't speak for the hate. I hate the emptiness that fills my mouth. The hunger that swallows it whole. *Fine*, I can say it. *I have herpes.* So what? Some people have Cancer. Some people have HIV. Those are the core shakers. The life changers. Those are the Cadillac of incurable diseases. Having herpes is nothing so very remarkable, or so he says. It's 'normal' – certainly not a core shaker or a life changer. From the outside, I'll still be me still Grace. But on the inside, something shifts. Something breaks.

"I understand how difficult this must be for you," Dr. Yu says, "but really it's not so bad, Grace. You can still have a perfectly normal sex life. You just have to be careful."

I murmur something that sounds like assent. *One in four people.* It is a lot. I certainly don't know any one in those four people, but it is a lot – at least, it sounds like a lot. And I'm sure that Dr. Yu does think he understands. After all, he seems like a nice enough man. But he doesn't. No one can. No one can understand how long the word forever sounds when you've still got forever to go.

CHAPTER EIGHTEEN

Across the table, my mom finishes her salad, having made short work of her burger. She eats daintily, intent on her pursuit, methodically munching away. I feel as though it's the first time I've studied her this closely since I was young. In this light, I can see that she is sixty and not forty, like I'd remembered. I can see that she is old. And it makes me sad for more than just myself. Which is a relief. A temporary reprieve. I want to say something to her. I want to say something, but I don't know how. Maybe I'm out of practice, or maybe I've never known how in the first place.

"Thank you," I try, realizing I'm much rustier than I'd thought. I have to clear my throat to let these words clear my lips. "Thank you for coming to get me. I appreciate it."

"Of course."

"And for not asking why when you did."

"Would you have told me?"

"Would it have mattered?"

"No," she says, "I would've come anyway."

"I know," I reply. It's only as I say it that I realize it's true. Which is precisely why I'd written her down in the first place. *In Case of Emergency*. I feel disloyal now – as though I owe her some explanation or show of gratitude for her unconditional *there*ness. "It was a man," I say. "I met him at work. Well, not at work – not at first – but he came there later."

She says nothing, allowing me to reconstruct the narrative noose from which I'd hung myself.

"He asked me out," I continue, "and I said, yes. I guess I shouldn't have. I guess that was stupid. He was a stranger, but I wanted to go. I liked him. And it felt nice. The attention, I mean. I thought it was a good enough reason to go. Well, and I liked him, of course. But you probably wouldn't have. He was a little older than me."

Her lips are set intently in her face. Her eyes set intently on mine. They ask me to go on. She does not, but they do.

"And now," I say, taking a necessary breath, one that's meant to steady the shudder that I know will break my next sentence in two. "And now, I have this thing…well, you already know. The doctor already told you…"

She waits. Makes me say it. Own it.

"He says I have herpes," I say. "I have herpes."

"And what about him?"

"Who?"

"The man you slept with," she says. "Did he tell you beforehand?"

"No," I say, "but then, I never asked."

"And if you had," she asks. "Do you think he would have?"

"I honestly don't know," I reply. "But what difference does it make? It's too late for that now." I stab my strawberry shake with my straw – plunging it deep into the pink goo. *It's true.* Jack doesn't matter. He's no one. Nothing. A mere speck of sand. Just the grain that enters the oyster's shell – changes the course of its life simply because it exists. It's the oyster who chooses to worry the grain into its sole reason for being.

"And now," she asks, "what will you do?"

"I don't know," I reply. "I can't think about that right now."

"What can I do?"

"I don't know," I say. "I can't think about that either."

"Well, what did Dr. Yu say?" she asks. "Did he give you a prescription? I can write one."

"He took a test," I say, "some swab. They're going to call me, but he says he's 99.9% certain. He gave me this." I pull the prescription from my pocket and slide it towards her across the table. She takes it. Studies it. Nods in assent. "Don't worry," she says, folding it in half and slipping it into her purse. "I'll take care of it."

I offer a weak smile. *Thank you.*

"And what about him?" she asks. "Have you told him?"

"He's away," I reply. "He'll be away. I'm not sure how long. It doesn't matter."

"I think it does," she says. "Don't you think you have a right to know if he was aware?"

"Why?" I ask. "It's over. I'm still not even sure what *it* was. But it's over."

She looks at me in silence, acknowledging the truth of what I say. She's a doctor. I don't have to tell her what incurable means. There are some hurts for which there is no healing. No prescription for the pain. No justice. No right. Only wrong. She knows. She taught me that.

"We'll get through this, Grace," she says, applying her standard-issue we-ing to something she can't possibly understand. "You'll live through this."

I laugh. Tilt my head back and allow my heart and my hurt to expand into my lungs – filling me with some vague approximation of lightness or levity. "Will I?" I ask. "And what then?"

"Life goes on," she says. "The same as it always has."

"Is that supposed to be comforting?"

"I don't know, Grace. These things – they don't make any sense. They just *are.* Fortunately, the human body is smart – it knows how to handle the hurt that seems too painful to survive."

"Oh, yeah," I ask, "how?"

"It dies," she says. "*Unfortunately*, that means that all the rest – the wounds you only think you can't sustain – they fall to the human spirit. It's terrible to think of, I know, but it's true. Everything seems hopeless right now, but you still have a choice."

"You're suggesting suffering as a choice?" I ask. "That's your professional opinion? As a doctor?"

"No," she replies, "acceptance. And I'm not speaking as a doctor, I'm speaking as your mother. It isn't about choosing suffering, Grace. It's about choice period. If you sit still in this sadness, I'm scared you'll never get out again. Life is full of a million *what if's*. A million unexpected twists and turns. Choosing to walk the path of one – even if it's wrong – that's what will get you to the other side."

"Of what?"

"Expectations, Grace. To experience. It's the moving that matters. The testing. Trying. That's what being young is all about. Freedom to choose. It's your life. It's up to you what you make of it."

Expectation. The word echoes through the tomes of my memory. Reminds me of a photo I'd found once in one of my flea market purchases. An image of a little boy – no more than four or five. He's standing alone in a grassy field, a sea of clouds kissing his brightly polished tow-coloured head. He faces the camera, close to a closed casket on a set of wooden girders. He wears a dark suit jacket, a tie and short pants. The afternoon sun glints off a freshly shined pair of shoes, and he squints against the light, a freckled nose screwed up against itself. One arm extended, the hand wrapped about the handle of the glossy casket as though it were the grasp of a guardian. My favourite part is the eyes – their expression. Like mine, they are a pale shade of ghostly grey; and, like mine, they are hooded by deeply expressive brows – the white smudges forming a sharply steepled question mark that meets in the middle of his forehead.

At the time, I decided that I would file this photo under *Expectation*. An amateur would spot the casket and guess *Grief*. But I'm no amateur. I know better. I knew it wasn't grief that gripped the child. He's too young for that. Grief requires the capacity to understand loss. To see the difference between what was and what will be – between the darkness and the light. But he is innocent – too young to comprehend the value of life or understand what his will become for the loss of it. It isn't grief that prematurely wrinkles his brow, but an almost apathetic sense of anticipation. His quizzical gaze not yet weary with enlightenment, nor riddled with the faint ripple of nervous apprehension. He's merely aware – cognizant of the fact that some aspect of his life has been forever altered, although he does not yet know how.

I like the photograph, and I like the little boy. I feel an affinity for him – for his young searching gaze, seeming to ask of the observer – seeming to ask of me – *What now?* At the time, I wished I could give him an answer. I wished I could take away his doubt. But the only comfort I could offer was in ownership. To give his moment a home – to let it be seen – safe. But now, thinking of this – thinking of him – all I can see is my own anger. My own hurt. My own grief. I had been there to protect him. *Who had protected me?*

My mother is still sitting across from me – silent, waiting – expectant. "I can't believe you," I snap. "This *just* happened – like…half an hour ago – I just found out. How can you ask me to make a decision right now? You're not being fair!"

"I'm not asking you to do anything," she says. "I'm only telling you what I know. Time is precious, Grace. Don't waste it in self-pity and self-doubt. Trust yourself. Trust yourself the way I do. And if you can't do that, then trust me. You'll get through this."

I swallow hard. My throat tight and dry. "And if I can't," I ask, "what then? How can I have sex when I'm contagious? You of all people should know that it's not safe – that *I'm* not safe."

"Grace, listen to me," she says. "This is something that happened *to* you. It doesn't have to define you. And you can get through it," she says, "that's what makes it so frightening – so painful." She covers my hand, limp and lifeless at the side of my plate, with her own – cool and composed, but warm and filled with warmth. She slowly withdraws it, letting it slide back across the table. "You know, I've never understood you, Grace. With Rachel, it was easy. We were the same. But you've always been a mystery to me."

"I've never wanted you to understand," I reply. "I only wanted to know that you loved me as much as you loved her – even if we weren't the same. Even if I couldn't be the way you wanted me to be. Couldn't be like Rachel."

"I do love you, Grace. Even without understanding you," she says. "Can't you see? It's not about that. It's about forgiveness. About how many times can you stand to offer someone your forgiveness, despite all your differences. I've never given up on you. Not once."

"What about dad, then?" I ask. "What about him?" She shakes her head. Purses her lips. "You know how that story ends, Grace."

"And me?" I ask, now even more frightened. "What about me?"

"What about you?" she asks.

"Do you forgive me?"

"Oh, Grace," she says, considering this a moment. She toys with the silver ring she wears on her ring finger. Now, on her left hand. Now, her right. "Can't you see? There's nothing to forgive."

CHAPTER NINETEEN

Ragged with fatigue, I slept then. Through the night on Friday. Into Saturday morning. Slept for what felt like forever in a fairy-tale trance. Sleeping Beauty. *Sleeping Broken.*

I open my eyes. Shut them tight. Remember. The past forty-eight hours playing out behind the curtain, a movie reel running on a continuous loop. I will it all to be a dream – a nightmare even. Anything but true.

I lie spread-eagled on the sheets. Breathe, and the taste of loneliness fills my lungs. My mother wanted to stay with me when she dropped me off, but I told her not to bother. I wanted to be alone, and I am. Have never felt so much so in my life. Bereft. Forgotten. Forsaken. Shipwrecked on the shores of myself.

Shores. I think of Jack then. Washed up on some obscure foreign French one. *What time is it there? What time is it here?* If I could move, I'd check. If I could move, I'd move on. Forget that I'd ever heard the word herpes. Forget that someone had ever been thoughtless enough to forget to tell me they had it. *Jack.* Probably sleeping at this hour, or sleeping with someone. And I, alone, softly spotlit by the first or last fingers of the sun. I feel sad. Disoriented. *Is it dusk or dawn?* It's too warm for dawn. Too cold for dusk. Too dark for day.

Rachel's room is quiet. Has the dark grey closeness of curtains shut against the falling light of day. I advance towards the dresser, stepping soundlessly, although I don't know who I am afraid of. The house is empty. Silent. Still.

I pull the token from my left pocket – a cheap bronze chain with a cameo dangling from it – the one from Faye's table. Subconsciously stolen – covered and coiled into my palm before I'd even known I'd done it. Before I'd even known I wanted to. Before I'd even known I had to.

I bring my closed fist to my mouth. Kiss the corrugated plane of my knuckles. Imbue the seemingly insignificant object with all the things I want to say but won't – at least, not now. I let it dangle and then fall, the weight of the piece causing it to spin in a few lazy concentric circles before pooling itself on the bare wooden surface. It isn't much but it will do. Rachel will see it when she returns. She will see it, and she will know what I mean. I know that she will understand. She will understand because she is my sister; and even if she does not, I know she will forgive me.

✧

I strike a match, and my nose fills with the faint smell of sulphur. Lighting a fire in the middle of summer seems silly – absurd even – but not when you feel as cold as I do. Not when you feel numb. Not when you're trying to get warm. Not when you want to watch things burn.

I touch it to the newsprint that pokes out from a pyramid of sticks – scraps of a basement wood box that hasn't been replenished since last winter. I don't know much about wilderness survival – just this – how to build a fire. I know how to open the flue so the room doesn't flood with smoke. I know because my father showed me how. He used to help me stoke the flames so I could roast marshmallows indoors on nights when my mom came home late from the hospital. He helped me jab the puffy whiteness on the ends of chopsticks left over from his Chinese takeout. Both items strictly contraband. I remember feeling happy. It was fun – fun to be a part of something private and prohibited. It was fun until it wasn't anymore. Until my mom came home. Then the fun would stop and the fights would begin.

As I said, I don't know much about wilderness survival; but, during those years, I learned a thing or two about domestic survival. I learned to hide – to make myself invisible – impervious to the ugly underside of family life. Ducked under the couch and peeked out from between the curved legs of carved wood, lying silently on my stomach, hands held over my ears. I focused on the dying embers of the fire – chopstick-skewered marshmallows dripping down over the smouldering tepee. I always stayed until the final refrain, not wanting to hear but not wanting to be away. Sometimes, I fell asleep beneath the couch and woke to find myself in bed. I was never sure who carried me or how. Only happy in the knowledge that I was found. Home. Safe.

Now, the greyed balls of newsprint catch the flame. They send bright licks of light up through the cracks and twine about the wood. I sit back on my haunches, crouching near the hearth. My skin still feels cold and clammy, but my face glows warm with the refracted rays of light. The fire grows slowly, the living room lit in an eerie incandescent glow that turns everything an unnatural shade of red – as though the building next door is burning bright with garden party Tiki torches or burning bright with burning down.

I fan the flames with a flap of my wrist, searching about me for a serviceable replacement for a strong gust of wind. On the coffee table, I spy the program from the concert – the cellist I'd taken my mother to see. I grab it, glancing at the glossy cover – an over-sized image of the instrument itself. I'm seized again with thoughts of its beauty, my breath catching in my throat as I think of his hands moving over its surface – Jack's moving over my skin.

Yes, it is beautiful. It is beautiful; and yet, it is mute. Incapable of singing when separated from its master – without whom it is merely an instrument. A tool. A pawn. And I think to myself then, *I should not wish to be a cello.*

Better to be free. *Better to be the song, than the strings it's played upon,* I think. Finish fanning the flames. Feed the pamphlet to the fire. I reach down, and drag the first of thirty-two boxes towards me. I start with Admiration. Feed the fire with one of one thousand photos, each one waiting to be kissed by the slow black burn of inevitable destruction, curling up in cruelly singed smiles that wither and wilt before they die. Disappear up the chimney. Into the night. Out to sea.

What has it all been for anyway, I ask myself, *this collection of happy thoughts – happy feelings.* From birth, we're taught how to feel, and how to name those feelings, but not all of them are good. Experience means being willing to let both kinds engrave themselves on our existence – etching out the emotional consequences of our choices in a way that spells permanence but doesn't foster regret. We don't get to choose. If we want to know happiness, we have to cut our teeth on sadness too. I can see that now, but still…*It isn't fair.*

I think of Jack then. Of justice and injustice. Right and wrong. Cause and effect. They say when a butterfly flaps its wings in one corner of the world, it can cause a hurricane in another. That's what they say at least. And maybe they're right. All I know is this. *My world is changed.*

My hand doesn't shake, and my will doesn't falter. I burn them all – every broken promise of eternal something-ness. Every last lie. Lies I can no longer live. Each image another failed option. Another dead dream. Each another male face. Each another *who.* Another of the millions of faceless nameless men in my future – the myriad of as-yet-unknown who's that

I will like and love and have to tell. The men who would be as disgusted with me as I was with myself. The men who would recoil in revulsion. The men who would run. All while I could not. Escape. And the only thing I can think – the only thing I can allow myself to feel – is indignant.

I lift the photo of the woman from the stack of waiting sacrifices. Hold it in my hand. Hold the heavy round smoothness of the sensation in my mind – *Desire*. It has a deliciously satisfying heft to it – promises to be enough – and yet, it's not. I run my fingers over the edge, firelight licking my palms with long orange tongues of flame. I find the cut from Friday. Try to slice a new track through the freshly healed skin with the serrated sides. It doesn't work, despite the fact I know it should. After all, even something as pleasant as desire has dangerously sharp edges. I know this now.

I think of my mother then, and our conversation from the night before. *When did you first learn you could live through the hurt?* I realize that I'd forgotten to ask her; and now, I want to know – if only because I know that I know absolutely nothing about her as a woman. Only as my mother. Nothing more. The photo slips from my grasp then, flutters to the floor. Inside, I feel the dam burst. The tears welling up behind my eyes with a force too strong to be countered. And I cry. Finally. Fully. Completely. I cry for the first time – a violent burst of sobs that leaves me gasping for breath. Without words. Only tears. Only fear. I do not cry for the magnitude of my situation, but for the smallness of it – each aspect of its impact so ordinary that I know I'll never be able to explain why it means not less than everything. And so, I cry for the futility of crying. And yet, I cry. I cry because I know my mother was right.

Acknowledgements

I'd like to acknowledge my family and friends, many of whom believed I should be writing long before I thought I could. This project is a testament to a blind leap of faith, and I appreciate all of your words of encouragement. I would also like to thank my editor and friend, John Calabro, for his patience, support and countless words of wisdom. Finally, thanks are owed to the entire Quattro team for the opportunity to work with a community of artists and writers who champion a unique Canadian literary experience. I am happy and proud to be a part of that tradition.

Other Quattro Novellas